Something about Julia made Kyle want to trust her.

Maybe it was the fact that her life wasn't as picture perfect as he'd first assumed. She'd had more than her share of pain, and yet Julia was still content with her life, even grateful for God's blessings in it. If only he'd learned years ago to be content and appreciative.

If he had any sense at all, he would keep a careful distance. Not only had he filleted himself and spilled his guts to her like a guy who *enjoyed* sharing, he'd almost taken a greater risk and told her the whole story about his arrest and conviction. What had he expected? That she would have believed his side of the story? No one else had.

Yes, he should be wary of Julia Sims.

Books by Dana Corbit

Love Inspired

A Blessed Life #188
An Honest Life #233
A New Life #274
A Family for Christmas #278
"Child in a Manger"
On the Doorstep #316
Christmas in the Air #322
"Season of Hope"
A Hickory Ridge Christmas #374
Little Miss Matchmaker #416
Homecoming at Hickory Ridge #453

DANA CORBIT

started telling "people stories" at about the same time she started forming words. So it came as no surprise when the Indiana native chose a career in journalism. As an award-winning newspaper reporter and features editor, she had the opportunity to share wonderful true-life stories with her readers. She left the workforce to be a homemaker, but the stories came home with her as she discovered the joy of writing fiction. The winner of the 2007 Holt Medallion competition for novel writing, Dana feels blessed to share the stories of her heart with readers.

Dana lives in southeast Michigan, where she balances the make-believe realm of her characters with her equally exciting real-life world as a wife, carpool coordinator for three athletic daughters and food supplier for two disinterested felines.

Homecoming at Hickory Ridge
Dana Corbit

Steeple
Hill®

Published by Steeple Hill Books™

STEEPLE HILL BOOKS

Steeple
Hill®

ISBN-13: 978-0-373-81367-4
ISBN-10: 0-373-81367-8

HOMECOMING AT HICKORY RIDGE

www.SteepleHill.com

Printed in U.S.A.

It was fitting to make merry and be glad,
for this your brother was dead, and is alive;
he was lost, and is found.
—*Luke* 15:32

To my sweet aunt, Sharon Hale. Though the miles separate us, I hold you close in my heart. You will always be my 'nother mother.

A special thanks to criminal defense attorney David Kramer, of the Kramer Law Firm in Novi, Michigan, for helping me navigate this story's legal maze. I so appreciate your help and support.

Chapter One

Bad habits died hard, that is, if they died at all. Kyle Lancaster understood that intimately after sharing living space with some repeat offenders who made the peccadilloes of his youth seem like child's play. As he stepped through the door of Hickory Ridge Community Church for the second time that day, Kyle needed no further proof that his bad habit of letting others talk him into crazy plans was alive and well.

He was working as a consultant for a new Michigan prison ministry—now *that* was an idea he never would have pictured. But then he never would have imagined himself inside a cell, either. And now he would never get the stench or the squashing feel of it out of his memory.

Kyle could understand why the Milford Area Ecumenical Council might want input from a real-life ex-con as it built its program, but he knew full well his brother, Brett, had only suggested him for the job to keep him busy and out of trouble.

Beggars couldn't be choosers, and he needed this job, at least for a while.

Halfway through a double-glass door, he stalled as the early May wind swirled past him into the building. Though he'd endured the meeting with the two ministers this morning, he wasn't sure he was ready to face the whole church community yet. He'd almost opted to delay the inevitable when a man and three women came up behind him.

Stepping to the side, Kyle held the door open for the other adults. The last one through the entry, the guy, surprised him by patting his shoulder. On instinct, Kyle whirled to face him.

Youth Minister Andrew Westin grinned as he held up his hands in the sign of the unarmed. "You came, after all."

Kyle gripped Andrew's extended hand. He was uncomfortable receiving help from anyone, but he was trying, with God's help, to be gracious in accepting it.

"There was a break in my social calendar." He didn't need to clarify that his whole calendar was blank.

"Well, I'm glad you changed your mind. I hope you're as hungry as I am. It's pasta night."

Kyle stomach growled but not loudly enough for

the youth minister to hear. "I've never heard of a church having Wednesday-night dinners."

"The choir director suggested it about a year ago. With all the church activities on Wednesday nights—children's choir, adult choir, the Deacon board and prayer meeting—some families were having a hard time fitting in dinner together. Now they can have dinner with the whole church family."

"Anyone can come? To the dinner, I mean." Kyle hated the insecurity he heard in his voice. He would have to get over worrying about what other people thought if he ever hoped to adapt to life on the outside.

Andrew studied him for several seconds before he spoke again. "Kyle, really, I wouldn't worry about the folks here at Hickory Ridge. This church is filled with sinners, not saints. Just the way it's supposed to be."

"Thanks for that, but—"

"Everyone deserves a second chance. I know I had one."

That last comment begged for elaboration, but before Kyle could ask any questions, Andrew started down the hallway leading to the Family Life Center. Andrew glanced over his shoulder at him. "Aren't you coming?"

Kyle followed gamely behind him. Maybe now wasn't the time to ask Andrew about second chances, but he would tuck his question away for later.

Loud voices and laughter escaped the gymnasium as Andrew pulled open the heavy metal door that separated the Family Life Center from the rest of the church. The aroma of garlic and oregano wafted along with the sounds.

Inside, a dozen long tables were lined with folding chairs to await the dinner crowd. Along the gymnasium's far wall, about thirty adults and children were in line, heading for the main serving counter with its roll-up metal window. At another table to the side, guests who already had plates of spaghetti or lasagna were serving themselves bread sticks and bowls of fresh salad.

"Hey, there's some food left," Andrew said.

As soon as he stepped in line behind a preteen girl with a mass of dark, curly hair, he gave the girl's ponytail a playful yank.

She turned around, a frown scrunching her cute face until she recognized the culprit. "Daddy Andrew!"

She flung herself into his arms. When he set her on the ground again, Andrew turned her to face his guest. "Kyle, this is my stepdaughter, Tessa." He gestured with his hand. "Tessa, meet Mr. Lancaster."

"Hi." She smiled shyly and turned back to her friends.

As they reached the front of the line, Kyle asked for a slice of lasagna and then made his way to the salad table. Only instead of a vat of iceberg lettuce and a pump container of French dressing like he was used to, he approached a spread with carrot shavings, cucumber slices, boiled eggs, croutons and sunflower seeds. Quantity and choices. There were even several dressings. He grabbed a second plate and started to build a salad, resisting the temptation to make a pig of himself.

"Excuse me, please. Coming through," a feminine voice called from behind him.

Kyle turned to see a blond pregnant woman holding a tray of fresh fruit. He set down his plates and lifted the tray for her, setting it on an empty spot near the end.

"Thanks." The woman grinned at him and then turned to look over her shoulder. "Is that the last of it, Julia?"

"I think so," answered a female voice as its owner pushed through the swinging kitchen door carrying a tray of brownies and cookies.

Kyle's breath caught as a raven-haired woman with a porcelain face like Snow White and Catherine Zeta-Jones combined came into view. No, neither the cartoon reference nor the Hollywood one did justice to that kind of perfection. Julia wore a low ponytail that fell in a silken stream to the middle of her back.

She glanced up at Kyle as she set her tray on the table, and her deep brown eyes widened, exaggerating their almond shape. For a moment Kyle thought he saw recognition in her eyes before her lush lashes swept down and she averted her gaze.

At the sound of Andrew coughing into his hand, Kyle started. *Snap out of it, Lancaster.* He was acting as if he'd never seen a beautiful woman before. Well, not up close in a long time, but still…

Andrew began introductions, but he indicated the blonde first. "Kyle, this is Hannah McBride. You already know her father, Reverend Bob Woods."

He set his plate on the edge of the table again so he could shake her hand. "It's nice to meet you."

Hannah indicated the brunette with a tilt of her head. "This is my friend, Julia Sims."

He smiled at Julia, balancing on the tightrope between looking and staring. She was attractive but not as perfect as he'd first thought. She wasn't particularly tall—no more than five foot four—and her curves were more generous than fashion-magazine wisdom demanded. He would have searched for additional flaws, but she smiled and he forgot why he was looking so hard.

"Julia, this is Kyle—" Hannah paused, waiting for him to fill in the blank.

"Lancaster," he supplied.

He hated that Julia's eyebrow lifted at the mention of his name. He hated even more that her reaction bothered him. Of course, his reputation had preceded him.

"Lancaster?" Julia asked. "Are you any relation to Brett Lancaster?"

"Brother."

"I thought you looked familiar."

So that was it. She'd only noticed a family resemblance when she'd looked at him. Maybe the whole church didn't know about his prison record, after all.

"You two do look a little alike," Andrew said. "Except for Brett's short hair."

"You know cops." Kyle shrugged, figuring his hair was plenty short enough. On reflex, his hand went to his neck. His hair barely covered it now, though a week ago it had been long enough to tie with a band.

Julia smiled again, an expression that lit up her whole face. "You must be such a proud uncle since Brett married Tricia and got an instant family. Brett is such a proud daddy."

Kyle tried to smile back and hoped he succeeded. "I can't wait to meet them."

"I didn't know Brett had a brother," Hannah said, tilting her head to the side and squinting as if trying to recall. "But I've met your sister, Jenny."

"She works in the hospital obstetrics ward with my sister," Julia added.

He had little time to ruminate on how everyone he'd met in Milford seemed to know everyone else, before Hannah posed the question Kyle would like to have asked himself.

"If you're visiting tonight, why isn't your brother here to show you around?"

Maybe for the same reason Brett hadn't even been by to see him since Kyle had moved into his downtown apartment over the weekend.

"Oh, I invited him," Andrew answered, covering the lingering pause. "Kyle's going to be working with our new prison ministry and helping out with plans for the Homecoming celebration. We want to familiarize him with some of the other church programs."

"The celebration's going to be great," Julia told him, excitement clear in her voice. "It's like a big family reunion for anyone who ever attended our church. We scheduled it on the same weekend as the Milford Memories festival—the second weekend in August. That way, former members can make a vacation out of their visit."

One of those cat-just-made-a-snack-of-the-canary smiles appeared on Hannah's face before she spoke again. "Andrew, have you told Kyle about *all* the church programs? What about our singles' program?" She turned to Kyle. "It's called Christian Singles United. Julia's a member. You should ask her about it."

Sure, Andrew had mentioned it, and Kyle had been quick to nix the idea. Still, though Hannah's approach had been about as subtle as a two-by-four to the head, Kyle couldn't resist sneaking a peek at Julia.

She rolled her eyes and frowned.

"Julia teaches first grade at Johnson Elementary," Hannah continued. "She's a great teacher and a great catch."

"Gee, thanks, Hannah." Julia shook her head, looking embarrassed.

"No problem. Now, Andrew and I are going to see if anyone needs help in the kitchen. You two enjoy your dinner."

She grabbed the youth minister's arm and pulled him toward the kitchen. Over his shoulder Andrew gave an apologetic shrug and disappeared through the swinging door.

When Kyle turned back to Julia, her light olive complexion had deepened to a pretty maroon, but she was too polite to cut and run.

"Sorry about that. You'll have to forgive Hannah. Ever since she got married a year and a half ago, she's been setting up everyone."

"I'll remember to keep my distance then."

Julia nodded as though she'd received the message that he wouldn't be a player in the local dating game. He had no business even thinking about the opposite gender, anyway. He had so much hard work ahead of him for the next few months. So much to prove.

"Well," she began again, "we still have to eat. So, do you want to..." She let her words trail away in an unspoken dinner invitation.

He glanced at his plates, all but forgotten on the salad table. "Sure."

As he collected his food, Julia reached for the brownies, placing two on a dessert plate. "Get your own," she said when she caught him watching.

He couldn't help grinning at her since she didn't have any dinner and was still making sure she didn't miss dessert. He had to respect a woman who had her priorities in order.

She led him to a long table, set down her plate, indicating for him to take the spot opposite hers. As soon as he took his seat, though, she hurried off to the serving table. When she returned, she was carrying a salad to go with her brownies.

"That's great that you'll be working with the Homecoming committee. Do you know which sub-committee you'll be working on? I'm on the Search and Invitation committee. We'll be trying to locate and invite as many former members as we can."

"I still don't know what I'll be doing for the celebration. They'll probably assign me where they need the most help."

She nodded, but he wondered if he saw disappointment in her expression. Instead of saying something more, Julia forked a bite of her brownie into her mouth and then started on her salad.

"So, you're a member of the singles' group." Kyle blinked. *Where had that come from, and how could he take it back?*

Julia lifted her head. "I guess you could say that." She chewed her lip before continuing. "But I'm not the best advertisement for it."

Kyle managed to keep his face blank, which was no small feat because in his opinion, a picture of Julia Sims would be exactly the kind of advertisement a singles' program could use. If group organizers wanted to attract new singles of the male persuasion, anyway.

"Why would you say that?" he asked.

"I've been a member for three years and I've never really, you know...met anybody."

"You're kidding."

She flitted her gaze his way but looked away again, something in her salad requiring all of her attention.

"Sure, I've *met* people," she began, still looking at the table, "but just no one special...for me."

"I still find that hard to believe." He also found it hard to imagine why he couldn't keep his mouth shut.

She looked up at him with a sheepish grin. "There were extenuating circumstances with a few of the men I met. In one case, my friend, a young widow, tried to set me up with this guy, and then she realized that God intended for them to be together."

"You mean...?"

"Yes. Tricia tried to set me up with your brother."

"You never went?"

Julia shook her head but was quick to add, "Brett never asked, either."

"Oh." His relief was more for Julia's sake than his own. His boring Dudley Do-Right brother would never have been a good match for an intriguing person like Julia Sims.

As if you would be.

"There were some others, too. Hannah tried to convince me to go out with her best friend, Grant. The only problem was that Grant was more interested in Hannah and hasn't dated anyone else since she got married."

Kyle shook his head, chuckling. "You're making this stuff up. It sounds just like a soap opera."

"It gets better. Tricia wanted me to go out with Brett's former partner, but she couldn't even convince him to *visit* the singles' group."

"Ouch." It sounded like a comic routine on the trials of dating in the new millennium—a regular comedy of dating-scene horrors—but he didn't tell Julia that.

"Yeah, ouch." She tore a corner off her second brownie and nibbled on it. "You see, if the church used me as an advertisement, Christian Singles United wouldn't look too successful."

"Those guys wouldn't come off looking too smart, either." The words were out of his mouth before he had the good sense to stop them. He was definitely out of practice talking to women.

Her cheeks reddening again, she glanced at the serving window, the salad table and the other dining tables to avoid looking at him. For such a lovely woman, she wasn't comfortable with compliments. That surprised him, but he suspected there were many surprising things to discover about Julia Sims.

Strange how he suddenly wanted to know more about her. Not the details he might find listed on some dating service data sheet or even the casual information fellow church members might know, but the deeper stuff. What made her nervous around him, especially if she didn't even know who or what he was? What made it so difficult for her to look him in the eye?

He shouldn't be curious. Rebuilding his own life would be enough like an uphill march after an ice storm without adding anyone else's dramas to the mix. But wisdom had never been one of his stronger points. He would have asked her some of his questions if someone hadn't entered the room then, announcing that prayer service would begin in ten minutes.

That announcement must have signaled the church greeters because several approached and introduced themselves, too many for Kyle to ever recall their names. Several asked questions, so he kept his answers vague.

The task would have been easier if he weren't so distracted by the woman who'd moved across the room to throw their trash away. Maybe he would give the singles' group a try, after all. At least it would give him something to look forward to besides meetings with his probation officer.

At the sound of the heavy gym doors opening, Kyle glanced over to see his brother in full Michigan State Police uniform, scanning the room as if he'd entered a crime scene. When his gaze landed on Kyle, Trooper Brett Lancaster took several long strides toward his table.

"I tried calling you tonight." Brett's words sounded more like an accusation than a statement. That he was staring down at Kyle the way he would a suspect during questioning didn't help, either.

Kyle glanced sidelong in the direction Julia had gone, and, sure enough, she now stood just a few feet away.

"I wasn't home."

"I'd gathered that. I wondered where you were."

What'd you think, a breaking and entering or a drive-by shooting? He pushed back his chair and stood. With effort, he calmed his breathing as he'd done so many times on the inside. He lowered his voice and leaned close to the brother he'd once admired.

"I'm not on a tether. I don't have to check in."

Kyle didn't expect an apology from his holier-than-thou brother, but Brett's stiff stance surprised him. Stepping back, Kyle crossed his arms and waited.

"I called Andrew a few minutes ago, and he said you were here."

"And you just drove right over?"

"I didn't figure—"

"What? That I should be here? At a prayer meeting dinner?" Kyle's eyebrows drew together as he studied his *big* brother. Though Kyle stood two inches taller than Brett's five-eleven and outweighed him by fifteen pounds, it was hard not to feel outsized by the ten-gallon hat that Brett wore.

Brett shook his head, appearing to search for the right words.

Kyle didn't give him time to find them. "I don't get it. You agreed to help me get a job, made a call about my apartment—" As realization dawned, he stopped himself, the stab of pain fresh though he should have been immune.

He stepped closer to his brother, too angry to be intimidated by the uniform and the badge. He spoke in a low voice. "Oh, I get it now. You're not upset that I work here, just that I'm here with these people."

"You're not making sense, little brother. And you're making a scene."

"As if you racing in here didn't make one?"

Brett gripped Kyle's shoulder, but Kyle shook off his hand and backed out of his reach.

"It's okay for me to live in town as long as I keep my head low. And it was okay for you to give me a recommendation at your church. I could work here as long as I stayed invisible. I don't know how you expected me to do my job that way, but that's not the point right now. I went too far by socializing here. You don't want your ex-con brother anywhere near your friends."

Trooper Lancaster's body became still, but he turned his head from side to side. Dread gripped Kyle's insides as he glanced at the startled faces around him. He'd forgotten their audience, and from the way everyone scattered and pretended to be involved in their own conversations he realized he'd been overheard.

Brett turned back to him, his eyes narrowed. "You're a one-man demolition team. You destroy everything in your path. Just like always."

"Maybe there's a quota. Only one perfect son per family."

"You're not worth it."

It was only a frustrated comment that Brett made under his breath, but Kyle didn't miss it. He lied to himself, saying it didn't bother him. Brett glanced around once more and then stalked toward the door. In his life, Kyle had never followed his older brother's example, but it didn't sound like a bad idea now.

He took two steps, catching Julia's image in his peripheral vision. A wave of melancholy filtered over him. It was best that she found out now, before she thought they could be friends or something. She didn't seem like the kind of woman who would be friends with a guy like him, anyway. The people around her probably had award lists…not rap sheets. None of that mattered. He didn't need friends. He didn't need anyone.

Still, one look at her wouldn't hurt. He turned his head toward her, hoping to steal a parting glance. He expected her to look away, to begin a conversation with someone else, to busy herself doing something—anything—so she didn't have to see him. But as his gaze touched her lovely face, she was doing none of those things. She was staring right at him.

Chapter Two

Julia stared into Kyle's wary hazel eyes, and she couldn't have looked away if a tornado had struck the church, collapsing the roof on all of them. The things Kyle and his brother had said to each other caused a powerful ache to build inside her, as if *she* had been a target of those hurtful words. Destructive words. Phrases that could never be taken back.

Kyle must have worn some protective armor to shield him from his brother's comments. At least it seemed that way since he wasn't watching the door through which his brother had disappeared but instead continued to stare at her as if daring her to look away. Did he think she was the kind of person who would go screaming in the other direction at the word *ex-con?*

Okay, he couldn't know what kind of person she was, and the term did make the hairs on the back of her neck stand up, but she didn't long for her running shoes. That Kyle worked at Hickory Ridge Community Church made this new information easier to digest. Reverend Bob and Andrew Westin would never have hired Kyle if his crime made him a possible danger to church members or their children.

With a silence in the room so profound she could hear her heartbeat in her ears, Julia waited while those eyes continued to study her. Sage eyes that had probably seen far more than she had in her twenty-seven years. He seemed to search inside her for something more than she could give. She wanted to believe she was above judging a person for his past, but it wasn't as easy as it sounded.

Still, Kyle looked away first. He glanced at the exit and then strode toward it, his hands striking the handle with a bang as he passed through the doorway. The door fell closed behind him.

Glancing around her, Julia found other church members watching the door as if they expected Kyle to reemerge through it. She doubted that would happen. He didn't know many people here. And from the scene they'd all just witnessed, he didn't even have a decent relationship with his brother, the only person in town he probably did know well.

Did he feel alone? She knew what that felt like. After her parents' deaths, despite her faith, she'd felt adrift while the rest of the world appeared solidly anchored. But Charity had been there for her. The half sister she'd barely known had reached out to her, even encouraging her to move to Milford so what remained of their family could be together. Who was there for Kyle? Who would draw him into a circle of friends? The answer was clear: he had no one.

Before her mind had the chance to rethink her plan, Julia hurried to the door. She didn't glance back, knowing curious eyes would follow her. Kyle needed somebody, and it didn't look as if anyone else was volunteering for the job. Even someone as apprehensive as she was had to be better than no one at all.

Her cross-trainers tripping along the carpeted walkway, Julia reached the outside only to find the parking lot quiet, the cars of families attending the prayer meeting and choir practice filling half the spaces.

Disappointment filled her. Maybe it was true what her father used to say about her: he'd called her a champion for underdogs, a collector of strays. Injured birds, lost kittens, new kids in town—they all ended up in a warm box inside the door or at their kitchen table.

This time none of that would be enough. Not enough to help a guy as scarred as Kyle likely was behind his armor. Rubbing her bare arms and wishing she'd remembered to grab her sweater, she started back toward the church entrance.

Somewhere behind her an ignition turned over, but the vehicle didn't start. Its driver tried a few more times, and the engine roared to life. An older model sedan backed out of its space, rolling toward the exit. As the car passed, Julia recognized Kyle in the driver's seat.

"Kyle. Wait." She rushed out so that he could see her waving her arms in his rearview mirror.

When she'd decided either he hadn't seen her or was pretending he hadn't, he stopped the car.

She hurried to the driver's-side window and waited until he lowered it. At first he stared straight ahead instead of at her. The breeze lifted a few strands of his tousled deep-brown hair. He wasn't wearing a jacket, and when he rested his elbow on the open window, his bicep strained against the cuff of his royal-blue polo shirt.

Finally he turned to look at her. "What do you want?"

"I wanted to see if you were okay."

"I'm great. Now you'd better get inside or you'll be late for prayer meeting."

She brushed away the suggestion with a wave of her hand. "I thought you might need someone to talk to."

"Didn't you hear enough inside?"

She didn't know how she expected him to react,

but the hard set of his jaw surprised her. Well, she didn't know much about Kyle Lancaster, but he had a stubborn bent as firm as his jaw.

"I guess I didn't," Julia said. She could be pretty stubborn herself when challenged.

His gaze flitted to her face and he pressed his thin lips together. "Then you weren't listening closely enough."

Julia rubbed her arms again, the chill this time coming from the man in the car rather than the spring breeze, but she refused to take his hint to back off. At least he hadn't closed the car window yet or pressed the gas pedal to the floorboard.

"I listened well enough to know that you're not getting much support from your one relative in town."

His hands gripped the steering wheel. "Thanks for coming out here, but I don't need your pity."

Julia lifted a brow. "Pity? I don't see anybody here pitying anyone else." She braced herself and steadied her voice. Doing God's work wasn't coming as easily to her as she would have expected. "I just thought you might like to go for coffee or something. You're new in town, and I thought you might need a friend."

He was shaking his head before she even finished her offer. "I'm not worth the trouble. Didn't you hear *Trooper* Lancaster?"

"I'm sure Brett didn't mean what he said."

"*I'm* sure he did."

His vehemence reminded her how little she knew about this family drama, and she felt properly put in her place. Her need to defend Brett didn't surprise her, as he'd always been kind to everyone in the years she'd known him. What did surprise her was the sudden impulse to defend his younger brother, as well. She barely knew Kyle, and what she knew for sure about him didn't inspire much confidence.

Still, Kyle Lancaster was a child of God, and he seemed awfully alone.

"I'm sorry." She rested her hands on the edge of the open window. She would have reached inside and patted his shoulder if she thought he would have let her.

"No big deal," he said, though it clearly was. "I don't need Trooper Lancaster or any of the Lancasters." He turned his head to stare out the windshield. "I don't need…"

He let his words trail away, but Julia still heard the word he hadn't spoken. *Anyone.* He didn't believe that, did he? As if he recognized her surprise and saw it as his opportunity, Kyle shifted his car into Drive and settled his hand over the automatic window control.

Taking his hint, Julia lifted her hands away from the window and stepped back from the car.

"Good night, Kyle. It was nice meeting you."

"Yeah, you, too. Goodbye." He glanced at her

once more, a strange expression lining his features, before he pulled the car down the church drive and onto the road.

Julia watched his car, a sense of loss building inside her. *I don't need...* His words invaded her thoughts again, as unsettling as when he'd spoken them. Her heart ached that anyone would have let him believe that was true.

Rubbing her chilly arms, she went back inside, but instead of joining the prayer meeting, she retrieved her belongings and headed out to her car. She wasn't in the mood to be in a social setting now.

Only after she'd parked in her one-car garage and had headed up the walk to her tiny but wonderful house on Union Street did Kyle's words came back to taunt her. He hadn't said "Good night" as she had. He'd said "Goodbye," as if he never expected to see her again.

The thought grated on her. Of course she would see him again. It was a small town. The village covered only a few square miles. And Kyle worked at the one place she frequented almost as often as her classroom at school: her church.

She hadn't planned to return to Hickory Ridge until Sunday services, but she decided as she turned her back-door lock that a visit to the church office tomorrow afternoon just might be in order. If she suddenly took an interest in working with the foundling prison ministry, she would raise a few eyebrows, but no one would be surprised to see her starting her Homecoming celebration work.

Okay, she would be getting a few weeks' head start on the search for former members, but it never hurt to be ahead of the ball, did it? If she happened to cross paths with Kyle Lancaster while she was there, then so be it.

Julia didn't want to wonder why she was trying so hard when he'd made it clear he didn't want anything from her. She might like to nurture others, but she'd never met someone who wanted her help less. He eschewed it and her. There were so many others she could help—her students, her church friends, others in the community—and they might even appreciate her efforts. Most of them didn't have an unspecified criminal record for her to be concerned about, either.

So why Kyle? The question reverberated in her thoughts. But he'd given her the answer even as he'd tried to push her away. She couldn't turn her back on him now even if she wanted to. Someone who didn't think he needed anyone might just need someone most of all.

Crouched on his hands and knees beneath his new desk, Kyle threaded computer cords through a hole in the back. He reached up to rub his aching neck that had no business being squeezed into that uncomfortable position.

He wasn't sure why Reverend Bob and Andrew

had insisted on putting one of the brand-new computer monitors on his desk. It wasn't as if he would be doing computer spreadsheets and video presentations in his job. At least, he hoped not.

For the most part, though, he knew what he was doing with stringing the wires. He'd done his share of troubleshooting the last few years on the dozen or so aged machines in the prison's computer lab. And before that he'd had some experience *unwiring* a few tasty electronics on the sly, but he chose not to remember those times now. He'd tried hard to put that life behind him, and it didn't do him any good to keep ruminating on it.

The cable Internet offered a bit more of a challenge, though. The prison's computer lab hadn't been connected to the outside world, so he was just learning about things like networks.

Even if he wasn't sure what to do with that blue cable, Kyle couldn't help feeling impressed with the quality of his work today. Something had to be said for good, honest work on the outside. His plan involved stepping stones, and this job was a solid first rock. He liked the idea that his work, even if he planned for it to be temporary, would help other prison inmates.

Pulling the excess monitor cable through the slot, Kyle secured it with a plastic tie. Something outside the desk made a loud crack, making him whack his head on the metal above him. Pain pulsed in the back of his head and dots of color danced inside his eyelids as he backed out from beneath the desk.

"Oh. Sorry."

The voice caressed his memory before Kyle even opened his eyes, so he had even more to frown about when he did. Julia grimaced as she stared down at him.

"You." He rubbed his head where it ached.

With a sheepish grin, she righted the wheeled desk chair that she'd knocked over, causing the commotion. "An accident. Honest. I didn't know you would be…" She let her words fall away, indicating with a sweep of her hand the boxes, wires and assorted tools of his project.

Coming up from the floor still rubbing his head, he sat on the seat she'd provided. "That I was a computer technician? Neither did I."

"Looks like you're handling the assignment."

"Something like that."

He tried not to notice, really he did, but Julia had this twinkle in her eyes and a smile that was impossible to ignore. As though she'd brought the sunshine right inside the building with her. That he could see that sunshine irked him even more. Neither spoke for several seconds, and Julia's gaze lowered to the floor.

Gingerly, Kyle came to his feet as the colored spots subsided. "May I help you with something?" He asked it to end the awkward silence but he still wanted to know. Especially since he'd all but waved his arms and insisted that she run in the opposite direction only yesterday.

"Uh, no. I just stopped by after school to pick up some things from the church office. Committee stuff for the Homecoming celebration," she was quick to add.

Noting her empty arms, he tilted his head to the side. "Did you get what you came for?"

She gripped those empty hands together, showing she hadn't missed the double meaning in his words, but she answered as if only one of those meanings had come to mind. "No. Not yet."

He leaned back in his chair and waited.

"Oh, and I thought I would stop by to see how you were getting on with your new job."

"Worried I would make off with the collection plates?"

"Should I be?" She raised an eyebrow as if daring him to come up with another smart-aleck remark. When he didn't, she continued. "I know how hard it can be starting a job in a new town where you don't know many people. I did that a few years ago."

It surprised him that he suddenly wanted to hear her new-girl-in-town story, but he didn't ask. "I'm doing fine, but thanks for checking." He indicated the mess of wires and tools. "One of the more glamorous aspects of my job."

"I get to convince first-graders not to pick their noses and to wash their hands after bathroom breaks."

"Sounds like fun." He almost wished they could stay here a while longer, trading clever comments, but she hadn't said what she really wanted. "I didn't expect to see you again after last night."

"Why not? You work in my church," she quipped before becoming serious. "I thought you might need a friend."

"I told you I didn't need—"

"Kyle, everybody needs *somebody.*"

"Well, I—" Realizing how ridiculous he sounded, he stopped himself before saying the word *don't.* Instead he crouched and started to pick up some of the computer packing material. Maybe he did need someone, but he wished he didn't. It would make his life a whole lot easier.

"Will you be working late today?"

Instead of answering, he tilted his head to the side, lifted a quizzical brow and waited.

"I thought I would try again to see if you wanted to go for coffee later."

"You don't give up easily, do you?"

"My dad always said I was as stubborn as a mule, but I'd like to think I've got the old gal beat."

He had to give her credit: she was tenacious to a fault. "If I agree to go later, will you let me get back to work? I want to finish this before I leave today."

"Then you might want to plug in the Ethernet cable for the network and turn on the router."

"I'll get around to it." And he would after she left

because he needed to go ask Andrew how those two particular items worked.

"Great. Do you want to meet downtown at about eight?" She fiddled with the keys dangling from her fingers.

"Sounds good. Don't forget your *committee stuff*. I didn't think you'd be starting on that for a few more weeks."

She shrugged. "You know. Early bird and all."

With a wave, she turned out of his office, heading toward the stairs. The paperwork she'd come for could probably be found in the main office downstairs anyway.

Kyle went back to work, wrestling a mess of wires into some order. As much as he focused on the task, though, his thoughts kept returning to Julia's visit.

He didn't know what to make of that, other than the obvious that she was a do-gooder in search of a project, but he didn't want to think about it right now. Analyzing it would make the whole coffee thing a bad idea. The anticipation flexing deep in his gut should have already given him a warning. Just coffee; it wasn't a real date, though his definitions might have blurred in the last few lonely years.

Those negative thoughts rankled him. Why couldn't he enjoy the fact that he was about to go for coffee with the most beautiful woman he'd seen this side of the television in more than three years?

Why did he worry about Julia's motives instead of just enjoying the moment?

He should have said no when she asked again. It had been hard enough asking his cop brother for a job reference. Now he had a woman turning him into a charity project. How much could a man's pride take?

Yes, he should have turned down Julia's offer, and there was still time to cancel, though he wouldn't kid himself by saying he would. A smile pulled at his lips as he realized she probably would talk him into going again, anyway.

The smile transformed into a frown as soon as the next thought crossed his mind. Sure, it was only coffee, only an opportunity to let Julia become the friend she so obviously wanted to be. That's where the trouble came in. Already, he could picture her sitting across from him with those shining eyes and warm smile. It would be hard to spend time with Julia, a woman who was too good for him on his best day, and not to wish the date were real.

Chapter Three

❧

Julia took her first sip of vanilla latte, closing her eyes and letting the sweet foamy milk at the top rest in her mouth before swallowing. "Hmm." Maybe if she focused on the drink instead of the company across the table from her, she could convince her hands to stop trembling. Why had she thought it would be a good idea to invite Kyle out for coffee? Who was she trying to convince that his ex-con status didn't bother? Kyle or herself?

"You say that now, but you'll be saying *grrrr* later tonight when you can't get to sleep."

When she opened her eyes, she caught Kyle grinning at her. "I ordered decaf, remember?" she told him.

Julia attributed her hurrying pulse to nerves rather than that potent smile.

"Never understood the point of decaf." Kyle took a long drink from his own double espresso.

"You'll understand when it's three in the morning and you're wide awake and reading your Bible instead of sleeping." Julia stiffened and looked at him sheepishly. She couldn't go around assuming that everyone got into Bible study, ex-cons or not. "Sorry."

"Why? Because I'll be missing all those ZZZs?" He studied her for a few seconds before adding, "Julia, I read the Bible. They allow the 'Good Book' behind prison walls. The wardens think it's better than Uzis or machetes."

"I didn't mean—"

But he brushed away her comment with a wave of his hand and took another sip of his coffee.

Julia frowned at the insulated cup in front of her. Great, now she'd insulted him by questioning his faith, based only on a criminal record. Kyle probably wished he'd stuck with his earlier refusal to go for coffee. She was fumbling for a way to backpedal when he set his cup aside.

"There were a lot of people at the prayer meeting dinner last night."

Relief filled her that he'd let her off the hook. "It was a nice crowd. Reverend Bob seemed pleased." She paused long enough to take another sip.

The door opened then, and a group of teenagers in Milford High School track warm-ups shuffled inside, bringing their rambunctious energy with them. Though the coffee shop offered plenty of background noise now, an uncomfortable silence settled between Kyle and Julia. As always, Julia wished she shared her sister Charity's easy way with people and fearlessness in social situations.

"So Hannah said you're a teacher?" Kyle said.

"Yes. The kids are great. So excited to learn. Ever since I was a little girl, I wanted to be a teacher."

"It had to be great figuring out so early on what you wanted to be when you grew up." He shrugged, a charming, boyish smile settling on his lips. "I've always been on the slow track in getting a clue."

"But you've figured it out now, right?" She sounded like Miss Mary Sunshine, but his words made her uncomfortable, and she wanted to help him see the bright side.

"You mean, the job at the church? Helping build the prison ministry is fine work for now. A step in the right direction. But definitely not something I want to be doing forever. I don't need the constant reminder."

She nodded, trying to see the situation from his point of view. She could see how it might be important to him to leave prison life behind him, and no matter how much he wanted to give back, the ministry would trap him in the past.

"You have something else in mind? Maybe something at Lancaster Cadillac-Pontiac-GMC?"

"How'd you know?" he began, then shrugged.

He must have understood that information traveled quickly in churches, especially when someone was looking for it. Until today, Julia had never realized that Sam Lancaster, the owner of the Bloomfield Hills auto dealership who used to do his own TV commercials, was Brett's dad, let alone Kyle's.

"Dad has to retire sometime," Kyle said. "And there's something to be said for a job where you wear a suit and don't have to get your hands dirty."

"I don't know. I think any job is fine as long as it's good, honest work."

She'd only meant to encourage Kyle in his present position, but as soon as the words were out of her mouth, she wanted to cram them all back inside. His tight expression told her he'd taken her comment the way she'd hoped he wouldn't: as if he were a criminal who needed to find *honest work*.

"Well, are you going to ask? Or have you already heard?"

"Heard what?" she asked, though she could guess since she'd led them right to this topic. Charity had given her some details about the Lancaster family's auto dealership and let her know that Kyle was twenty-eight, the youngest of Sam and Colleen Lancaster's three children. Even Charity hadn't known the specifics about Kyle's conviction, though. Brett always had been tight-lipped about his brother's incarceration.

Because Kyle crossed his arms and waited for her to give him a better answer, she gave up pretending she didn't understand what he meant. "I haven't heard."

"You have to wonder. I might be a danger to society. A murderer? Or terrorist? You're probably worried now whether you should have met me here."

She bristled that his guess was close to being on target. "If you were a danger, you wouldn't be working at my church."

"Okay, I'll give you that one. But you still want to know."

After a few seconds under his stare, so intense he could have been studying the capillaries beneath her skin instead of its surface, she shrugged. "I'm curious. But don't tell me…unless you want to."

Kyle picked up his coffee and swirled it around, though he hadn't put anything in it that would require stirring.

"It's a matter of public record, but I'll save you the trouble of hunting it down. Felonious assault. Felony possession of stolen property. Felony possession of a firearm." He ticked off his charges on his fingers as if he were used to repeating them. "The first two are five-year felonies, served concurrently, but the last one came with a mandatory two-year sentence."

"You were in prison five years?"

"No. Just the mandatory two, plus another one for good measure. I'm on probation now, so if I mess up, I get to head back to the lovely Thumb Correctional Facility in Lapeer."

"You're not planning to go back, right?"

"Nah. Three squares a day were good, but—" He quit his joke mid punch line, becoming serious. "No, I don't want to go back. Ever."

"Is there a story that goes along with those charges?" She hoped it was a mitigating story. The thought of Kyle holding a gun wasn't making her feel warm and fuzzy inside.

He studied her for several seconds and then shook his head. "There is, but it's a long one. Another time."

Julia nodded, pleased he'd opened up to her as much as he had. He might have wanted to say more, but they didn't know each other well. She would solve that problem by getting to know him better, even if he did make her nervous.

She was relieved when he changed the subject and asked about her sister.

"Did you two grow up in Milford?"

"Charity did. With her mother."

"You're half sisters?"

Julia couldn't help smiling as her sister's image filtered into her thoughts. "If you'd met her, you would have wondered about that. We have different mothers. We look a little alike, but in our hair and coloring, Charity's as light as I am dark."

"Like my brother and me, huh?"

He was trying to be funny, but his words rang flat in her ears. He'd made several comments like that today, seeming to wield self-deprecating humor like a shield. It bothered her that he thought he needed to protect himself from her judgments.

When Julia didn't make another joke at his expense, as he seemed to expect, he leaned forward. "You were saying about your sister…"

"I was in college before I ever learned that my father had an ex-wife and another daughter."

The surprise in his eyes reflected some of the shock she'd felt when her father had first told her. She couldn't begin to describe the sense of betrayal that accompanied the revelation.

"That had to be a shock," he said. "Your mom didn't tell you, either?"

Julia shook her head. "She always knew, but she thought it was Dad's place to tell me. Mom had already been gone a few years—complications from diabetes—when he finally did tell me."

"That's tough. You must have been furious with your dad for keeping the truth from you."

"Sure, I was at first. As mad as Charity, though she had more reasons to be angry. Dad hadn't fought harder to find her when her mother had disappeared with her. Charity's mother even told her that her father was dead, so she had that lie to deal with, as well."

Kyle shook his head. "How does anyone get past that?"

"With God's help, we can get over anything, don't you think? Besides, everyone deserves forgiveness. Everyone deserves a second chance. I'm just glad we all started to heal before it was too late."

"Too late?" His eyes widened as if he could already guess the answer.

"Five years ago, just a year after Charity located Dad, he passed away. But at least they had the chance to get to know each other. I got to know my sister, too. We attended Charity and Rick's wedding together, and Dad was so proud."

"How'd he…"

"The doctors said it was a heart attack, but I think it was from a broken heart. He never got over losing Mom."

Kyle shook his head, an incredulous expression on his face. "And here I figured your life was downright—"

"Perfect?" she finished for him. "Nobody's life is that. God allows us all to experience trials, but He gives us the strength to survive and even thrive."

He grinned at her. "Has anyone ever mentioned that you're a bit Pollyanna?"

"I prefer to think I'm an optimist."

"Okay, an optimist. Still, your life hasn't been the stuff of a Frank Capra movie. How did you keep that positive attitude?"

"I haven't always had one, especially on those dark days. Like when Mom's blood sugar was so out of whack that an ambulance was always in our driveway. We prayed constantly, but there was nothing any of us could do for her."

His understanding gaze unsettled her, as if he'd heard more than she'd said out loud. She didn't like being that transparent. She wondered if Kyle could see how conflicted she'd always felt over her mother's illness—helpless to take her mother's pain away, sometimes resentful of the burden her mother's disease had placed on the family and guilt-ridden over her resentment.

"Well, as you said, God helped you to survive—no, thrive."

He smiled as he said the last word. The wariness that she'd seen in his hazel eyes the other night had been replaced by warmth so pervasive that her cheeks heated under his study. Did he like what he'd seen? Did he find her pretty? It shouldn't matter what he thought, but there was no denying that it did. Butterflies seemed to continually take off and land on runways inside her belly.

"That's me, a thriving lady," she choked out.

As he continued to watch her, Kyle tilted his head forward and a lock of his unruly hair fell over his eye. The impulse to reach out and brush his hair aside surprised her so much that she glanced over his shoulder to break the connection. She grasped for the safety of their earlier subject.

"About surviving, I've been blessed to have

Charity and Rick around. They've helped so much. You know how important it is to have the support of family—"

Julia stopped herself, but she could see from the way Kyle shifted that it was already too late. How could she have forgotten, even for a second, that Kyle didn't have supportive family members like her sister and brother-in-law in his life? Kyle needed a friend—not a girlfriend—to help him readjust to his new life. They were here for that reason alone, and she needed to remember that.

"Yeah, I know." He must have read the confusion in her gaze because he continued. "I had the most supportive parents who ever lived. Somebody should have given them a few medals for dealing with a son like me. But there's only so many times parents can bail their kids out before they start losing enthusiasm for it."

"Have you seen them since you've been… well…?"

"Out? No. They didn't visit me on the inside, either."

"That's terrible!" Julia glanced around the coffee shop that had suddenly become quiet. At least the high school track stars had long since headed home, leaving only a few straggling customers sitting around the room. When she turned back to Kyle, he was shaking his head.

"Now don't say that. I deserved worse for all I

put them through. Even as a teenager, there wasn't a party anywhere in Bloomfield Hills that I wasn't smack in the center of. Partying, girls, joy rides in *borrowed* cars—you name it.

"Mom and Dad bailed me out each time, hoping it was only a phase. And I promised every time I would do better. After the last arrest, I guess I wore out my last second chance."

"They gave up on you?"

"Wouldn't you have?" He moved his paper coffee cup back and forth between his hands.

She mulled over it for a few seconds, but she had to admit the truth. "Probably."

"Mom still wrote to me every week, but she told me she and Dad couldn't bear to see me behind the glass."

Julia sipped down the last of her coffee that had long since gone cold. It broke her heart to think his parents weren't on his side, either. "Are you afraid you'll never earn their respect again?"

"I don't know—"

"You'll do it. Don't worry."

At first he looked surprised by what she said, and then his gaze narrowed. "I have a lot to prove. To a lot of people. It's something I have to do alone."

Before she had a chance to answer, an announcement came over the loudspeaker saying the coffee shop was about to close. Julia glanced around, surprised to see that the other stragglers had left, leaving only them and a few staff members who looked anxious to get home.

Tossing their empty cups in a trash can, Kyle and Julia stepped out into the main part of the shopping center and started down the stairs toward the parking lot behind the building. After all the details of their lives they'd shared tonight, a strange silence settled between them. Was Kyle sorry he'd opened up to her?

After an awkward goodbye, they both climbed in their cars and pulled out of the lot. As Julia drove through the deserted streets toward her house, Kyle's words filtered through her thoughts again. Yes, he did have something to prove, and from what she could tell, it would be a challenging job.

But he'd also said that proving himself was something he needed to do alone. And he could do it without help from anyone else. She could see that now. He seemed to have an inner strength she hadn't recognized in him at first.

Yes, he could face this challenge alone just the way he'd been in his prison cell, but there was no reason he had to be. Alone, that is. He could take a friend along for the ride, and she was volunteering to embark on the journey. She could even help him repair the broken relationships with his family, too, if he only gave her the chance.

Kyle settled back on the well-worn plaid sofa and closed his eyes. Only that dated piece of furniture, a tiny television, a mismatched card table set and a mattress and box spring—all appreciated gifts from anonymous Hickory Ridge church members—filled his downtown studio apartment, and yet it still managed to look cramped.

"Bigger than a prison cell," he mumbled, reminding himself to be grateful.

He wouldn't have this tiny space and a door that opened at his will if he hadn't received probation, and more than that, he wouldn't have had a chance to close down the coffee shop with Julia Sims tonight. He should have been thrilled on both of those counts, particularly the part about sharing the evening with a beautiful woman. Yet a seed of discontent had been growing inside him from the moment they'd walked out of the coffee shop and he'd climbed inside his junker of a used car to drive to his apartment. He couldn't explain it. They'd had a nice time together, even if he'd recklessly shared more with her than he'd told any of his fellow inmates in thirty-six months at Lapeer.

He should have known better, but something about Julia made him want to trust her in a way he hadn't trusted anyone in a long time. Maybe it was the fact that her life wasn't as picture-perfect as he'd first assumed. She'd had more than her share of pain, and yet Julia was still content with her life, even grateful for God's blessings in it. If only he'd learned years ago to be content and appreciative.

But more than his respect for her, Julia's confidence in him appealed to him more than it should have. She seemed confident he would be able to earn his family's respect. How could she be so certain when he was anything but?

If he had any sense at all, he would keep a careful distance from her. Not only had he filleted himself and spilled his guts like a guy who *enjoyed* sharing, he'd almost taken a greater risk and told her the whole story about his arrest and conviction. What had he expected? That she would believe his side of the story? No one else had. And what difference would it make if she did believe him?

Yes, he should be wary of Julia Sims. She was one of those people who needed to "fix" other people, and she'd made him her current project. Though her need didn't offend him anymore because he understood that it came from her own scars, he still had to be cautious.

Frustration filling him, Kyle planted his feet on the floor and leaned forward, resting his elbows on his legs and his head in his hands. Why did he insist on lying to himself? His ennui didn't deal with any of his excuses, though they all contributed to it. Something else entirely had climbed under his skin and refused to budge.

While they were sharing coffee and their sad stories, just for a moment he'd been tempted to see more than was really there between them. He'd thought that another time, another place, if he were someone else entirely, he might have had a chance with Julia Sims.

Chapter Four

Kyle closed his office door and started downstairs to the main level on a Friday afternoon more than a week later. This part of the church wasn't newer construction like the vestibule and the sanctuary, but it had its own charm. The two-story section was part of the stately home that once housed all of the church's programs.

He liked the statement that the structure made: it showed a commitment to the church's roots even as the congregation grew. He'd found a lot of things to like about Hickory Ridge in his first week of working there, though, admittedly, he hadn't made much progress on the development of the prison ministry. Reverend Bob had assured him they were still working out some final details for joint funding of the ecumenical ministry.

Since waiting wasn't one of his more developed

skills, he itched to make some progress. The sooner the program was well established, the sooner he could leave it to more capable hands.

Today would be another day of negative progress toward that goal. He knew that. And it should have frustrated him more than it did, but he didn't bother kidding himself that he minded. *She* would be there. Okay, he didn't know for sure, but she might.

He hadn't seen Julia at all since Sunday services, and even then they hadn't had time to talk when he'd sneaked in late and slipped out right after the benediction to avoid another confrontation with Trooper Lancaster. He'd avoided Wednesday prayer meeting for the same reason, though he'd wondered if she might have been there.

So today when Reverend Bob had assigned him to work on the same committee Julia had mentioned before, he'd looked forward to it more than he had any business doing. Even lecturing himself about it hadn't stopped the anticipation he felt as he entered the main office.

"Hey, Kyle." Hannah waved from behind the counter. "Need something?"

"Just the paperwork for the Search and Invitation committee."

"Oh, you'll be working with that? Julia took a lot of it home, but there are a few files in the storage room."

Hannah indicated with a tilt of her head a doorway behind her, the smallest smirk on her lips. Kyle moved around the counter and headed in the direction she'd indicated.

He couldn't help being disappointed that the room was empty. Just as well, he decided. At least he could focus on this new assignment and not on Julia. On a long folding table, several large brown accordion envelopes had been arranged, one for each of the subcommittees Reverend Bob had mentioned. He claimed the one for the committee he'd been assigned to and unwound the string holding its fastener closed.

He hoped Julia had a lot of the materials at home because the contents looked a little sparse. Still, he pulled out a manila folder and tucked the container under his arm. He could do Internet searches from his own desk PC upstairs.

Trying to balance the file with his free arm while opening the folder in his hands, he crossed back through the office and out the door.

"Find some interesting reading?"

Kyle glanced up toward the voice he recognized, somehow managing to avoid scattering the file over the floor. Julia grinned at him.

"It's not *The Grapes of Wrath,* but it'll do."

Their gazes connected the way they had before, but this time Julia was the first to look away.

She looked back at him, or, more specifically, at the labeled file under his arm. "Hey, we're working on the same committee."

"For a few weeks, anyway. Who else will be working with us?"

"Reverend Bob and Andrew oversee all the committees, but I'm doing most of the search work myself."

"No wonder they thought you needed some backup."

"It's not that bad. Just doing Internet searches for past members in whatever city or state they were thought last to have lived. Members keep e-mailing, too, with updated info."

"Sounds like a lot of work to me, but whatever you say. I'll let Reverend Bob know you've got it handled."

She appeared to consider that for a few seconds and then shook her head. "I don't mind the help. The searches haven't all been as easy as I expected, especially for families with names like Smith."

"Or Woods," he observed, supplying the minister's surname.

"And I've discovered that a few of our former members have moved more than once."

"What happens if you can't find them? Have you accepted that you might not locate some of them? That some might not even *want* to be found?"

"Want to?" Her eyebrows drew together. "Why wouldn't they want to? We don't have big battles in this church."

Kyle shook his head. "You're right. Forget I said anything."

Good thing she seemed satisfied with his answer because he wasn't sure how he would explain what he'd said. Just because there were people in his life who would prefer to stay hidden didn't mean everyone was like that.

"How about we divide the list and work individually on the easy searches?" she said. "We'll tackle the tougher ones together."

"Sounds good. But no lists were in the file."

She grinned sheepishly. "Right. I took the list home to work on in the evenings. I'll get your half to you."

He was marveling again that Julia didn't have more dates to fill her evenings when she snapped her fingers.

"I know. I'm going to a picnic at Central Park with my sister, Charity, and her family. Why don't you join us? I'm sure they wouldn't mind. I could give you the list then."

"I don't know." He wasn't even sure why he hesitated when he had to admit he'd been looking forward to seeing her.

Still, as tempting as spending an afternoon with Julia sounded, there was something about her invitation that appealed to him more. Julia had mentioned the word that had meant little to him in the past but had become so critical now: family. He wasn't ready to face his judgmental brother again, and he hadn't gotten up the guts up to visit his parents since his release, but he still liked the idea of sharing time with somebody's family.

"I guess that sounds all right," he answered.

"Oh, good. It's going to be fun."

"Your sister's family? Does that include her mother?"

At first she looked surprised, but then she must have remembered that she'd shared the story because she shook her head. "I'm sure she was invited, but she tends to decline when I'm invited, too."

"Her loss."

She smiled at that, but sadness lingered in her eyes until she perked up again. "I hope you like cold fried chicken, German potato salad and apple pie. Charity's an amazing cook."

"What about you?"

"If you like boiled water, I'm your cook, but otherwise you might want to consider takeout. I usually survive on frozen dinners and canned soup."

"Nobody can be everything, I guess." He said it as a joke, but he was serious. A Julia Sims who was also a twenty-first-century Julia Child in the kitchen might be too much for Milford, Michigan, to handle—in his part of town, anyway. He didn't mention that or the fact that once upon a time he'd been more than competent with a sauté pan and spatula.

Fidgeting, she tilted her head to the side. "So, we'll meet you there tomorrow at about noon?"

"Need me to bring anything?"

"Just yourself."

"I'll be there. I'm looking forward to it."

He smiled at her, and she smiled back for several seconds before looking away shyly.

"I'd better get going. See you tomorrow." With a wave, she started for the door.

Kyle studied her as she left. Why had Julia come to the church in the first place? If she'd come for her committee work, she hadn't brought anything, and she hadn't taken anything with her. He didn't mind the idea that she might have come just to invite him to the picnic. It was a kind, Christian gesture for her to include him. It also beat a Saturday afternoon of him sitting around his apartment wishing he had cable.

Anyway, there was something to be said for fun, food and family on a sunny afternoon. Though he realized it was unwise, he couldn't resist imagining himself slipping away with Julia for a romantic walk along the river. And maybe it wouldn't be a bad idea for him to become involved with a woman right now. He was looking forward to tomorrow, all right. He couldn't wait.

"Would you stop fidgeting?"

At her sister's voice, Julia looked up from her hands that were indeed fidgeting. In fact, the wrestling match of her wringing hands had become downright painful.

"What do you mean?" Julia asked, but couldn't keep a straight face.

Charity frowned at her, but her expression didn't stick, either. She slipped onto the picnic table bench across from her younger sister. "Don't worry. He'll be here. Nobody skips my fried chicken."

"That's not what I'm worried about."

Nodding, Charity glanced over Julia's shoulder to the parking lot. "I wondered about your plan. It'll probably be fine, though. He'll appreciate the effort."

Charity's uncomfortable expression suggested she wasn't as confident as her words. Julia tried not to let her sister's unease shake her confidence, not when she knew she was doing the right thing.

Rick called out to his wife from the blanket just outside the park shelter. "Hey, Charity, take a look at this."

Both women looked up in time to see ten-month-old Grace take an unsteady step toward her daddy. The tiny golden ponytail on top of her head bounced with the effort of this new skill, but her eyes shone with excitement. The next three steps came in a rush before she landed on her diaper-padded behind. With a wail, the baby held out her arms for her mother.

"When it's playtime, she wants Daddy, but when something hurts, it's all Mommy," Charity said, already off the bench and gathering her child in her arms.

"She just knows which of us gives softer hugs." Rick grinned as he leaned down to wipe a tear from his daughter's tiny pink cheek.

Charity glanced toward the parking lot again. "Oh, he's here."

Swallowing, Julia looked over her shoulder to determine which *he* had arrived first. Kyle had climbed out of his car and was reaching back inside it for something.

Julia took a deep breath to steady her nerves, but it didn't help. Somehow this didn't seem as good an idea as when she'd come up with it yesterday, and not just the surprise part, either. She'd hoped to develop some immunity to Kyle by now. She'd kept her distance for a whole week, figuring time and space would help her put her thoughts about him into perspective. Kyle was the kind of man she should be willing to reach out to as he tried to repair his life, but he wasn't the type she could ever see socially. Unfortunately, his past did make a difference.

So why, if she realized he was a poor choice for her, couldn't she stop these feelings of attraction she felt whenever she was around him? Even now as she watched him bend to pull several shopping bags from his car, she couldn't help noticing how his polo shirt stretched across his shoulder.

The shirt's deep green color would bring out the

flecks of green in his hazel eyes. She wished she didn't know that.

Glancing to the side, Julia discovered that Charity had come to stand beside her and now balanced Grace on her hip. Julia could only imagine what she'd seen because that knowing smile Charity wore was something only a sister could love.

Julia couldn't meet her sister's gaze. "I told him he didn't need to bring anything."

"That's what I told you, too, and look at how well you listened."

The bags of bakery goods from where she'd pillaged the local Kroger's spoke for themselves, but still Julia explained, "I just didn't want us to run out of food."

Kyle started in their direction, his saunter confident and unhurried. Julia liked seeing this self-assured side of him, so unapologetically male.

"That's unlikely."

"What's unlikely?" With effort, Julia drew her attention back to her sister.

"Like you said. That we'd run out of food." Charity indicated with a tilt of her head the picnic table they'd commandeered and then loaded with enough picnic fare to feed a small army—or at least a start-up militia.

"Oh. Right."

Kyle had reached the edge of the parking lot, so Julia waved to make sure he'd seen them. His smile was so warm that she felt rooted in place by it with no thought of anything but staring back at him.

"Hi, there," he said when he reached her.

"Hi."

Kyle looked at the shopping bags dangling from his hands. "I didn't want to show up empty-handed."

"Thanks. Here, let me get those." Rick stepped forward and relieved him of the bags, setting them on the picnic table bench.

Julia cleared her throat. "You met my sister and her husband at church, right?"

"Not formally."

Charity jutted out her hand. "Well, let's fix that. I'm Charity McKinley." She paused to grip his hand. "That's my husband, Rick."

The two men shook hands, and then Rick indicated the baby his wife held. "And this little mess-maker is Grace."

Kyle studied Grace, who was giving him a stranger once-over. "She looks clean to me."

"Give her a few minutes," Charity said with a chuckle. "We tried to introduce ourselves at church on Sunday, but you were gone so fast. You must have been in a hurry."

The side of his mouth lifted. "Something like that."

Charity and Rick exchanged a look, but neither said more. Grateful that they didn't, Julia flitted a look toward the parking lot. Maybe her other guests had decided not to come, after all, and maybe that was just as well. Charity had suggested it might be too soon, and she was probably right.

Rick lifted Grace from his wife's arms and swung her around until she giggled. "I don't know about the rest of you, but I hate to see all of this food go to waste."

"Go to waste? Are you kidding?" Kyle gave her a look of pure incredulity with a touch of mirth. "We can't let that happen, now can we?"

"So let the food frenzy begin," Julia returned.

Julia could feel herself relaxing for the first time since she'd pulled into the lot of Central Park. Now she would get the chance to enjoy the afternoon—the sunny day, the breeze off the Huron River, the swings inside the playground. Even the company.

She couldn't help grinning as she watched Kyle, paper plate already in his hand, examine the spread Charity had laid out for them. He fit in so well with her family. He laughed with Rick as if they were old pals. Charity liked Kyle, too, if the way she followed him around the table and plied him with food was any indication. Even Grace had bestowed on him one of her precious smiles, from the safety of her mother's arms.

She could get used to this, even if she and Kyle were only friends. Even if she would have to keep reminding herself that the rest of the day.

"Hey, Julia," Rick said in a stage whisper from the corner of the shelter. He mouthed the words "He's here."

This time she didn't even have to look to know which *he* her brother-in-law was talking about, but she glanced in the direction he indicated, anyway. Her stomach tensed as she caught sight of Brett carrying a covered casserole dish in one arm and a basket of something else in the other. Behind him, Tricia carried Anna, the couple's seven-month-old baby, her nearly bald head protected by a colorful sun bonnet. Taking up the rear were Lani, Rusty Jr. and Max, Tricia's children with her late first husband.

Brett grinned when he saw Julia. Max waved, causing him to drop the lawn chair he carried. The family laughed as Lani helped her little brother reclaim his load.

Julia knew the instant Brett recognized Kyle because his laughter died and his smile disappeared. He stopped so quickly that Tricia bumped into the basket he carried and then looked up at him, surprised.

Swallowing with difficulty, Julia glanced sidelong at Kyle. He stood frozen in place, his jaw ticking as if he was clenching and unclenching his teeth. Shock and fury clashed in eyes that he trained on his brother. He let the plate in his hand drop to the table.

The children ran up behind their stepfather and then stopped, looking back and forth between the two men. Julia started to do the same thing, but when she looked back at Kyle, he had turned those angry eyes on her.

"Julia, would you mind telling me what Trooper Lancaster is doing here?"

Chapter Five

Kyle posed the question, but he didn't bother waiting for the answer. He had a pretty good idea what it was, anyway, and he didn't want to hear it. He'd only felt set up like this one other time, and he'd had a nice orange jumpsuit and a cell of his own for that one.

But he couldn't think about that, not now when his brother was standing there, looking as furious to see him as Kyle was to be broadsided by Julia's meddling. His own anger propelled him toward Brett.

"What are you doing here?" he asked from between gritted teeth.

"Same as you. I was tricked."

Brett looked different out of uniform—less intimidating—though even in jeans and a T-shirt he still had a rigid bearing.

"No other reason to be within thirty feet of the family embarrassment," Kyle chided.

Brett shook his head. "Let's not go into that again."

"Why not? Because your family's here to see it? The family you haven't even bothered to introduce to me though I've been in Milford two weeks."

He stopped and turned to the woman and children standing next to his brother. "Oh, hi, guys, I'm Uncle Kyle."

No one responded, but Tricia's three children stared up at him, wide-eyed. The youngest boy's mouth hung agape. Ashamed, Kyle was grateful that at least he hadn't referred to himself as *Uncle Kyle the Jailbird* or something. These kids couldn't help who their stepfather was, so he shouldn't have involved them.

Brett stepped forward, putting himself between his family and his younger brother. "You haven't been beating down my door to see me, either."

"Why would I? You think I need this abuse?"

"Well, wouldn't want you to have to put up with any criticism after the perfect life you've led. A real example. Just the person I want around my kids."

"Can't you see—forget it. You'll never change."

"That's a laugh, coming from you."

Kyle fisted his hands at his sides, bitterness welling within him. He could have told Brett that he wasn't the same man who went into prison three years before, that he'd become someone that just maybe even Brett could respect, but now he was too angry to try.

"Glad I could entertain you."

"Buddy, your antics stopped being funny years ago."

"Enough." Tricia stepped in front of her husband, her presence surprisingly commanding despite her petite size. She raised a hand to stop the conversation. "You two have to stop this."

"Don't worry. I'm done," Brett said with a frown. He looked past Kyle to the Sims sisters. "I'm sorry about this. Thank you for inviting us, but I think we'd better leave."

He stepped to the table, lowered the dishes his family had brought for the picnic and then, lifting the baby from Tricia's arms, ushered his family to their car. The children kept peeking back, but they didn't ask questions.

"That didn't go well," Julia said as she watched their car pull back out onto Main Street.

"Ya think!" The words came out louder than he planned, but Kyle didn't care. What she'd done was wrong, and she needed to know it. He closed the distance between them. "What were you thinking inviting Trooper Lancaster here?"

Julia stared at the ground. "I just thought if I got the two of you together—"

"That we'd start up again in front of my brother's whole family? I'd never even met those people before. Well, I hope you got the show you were looking for." He gritted his teeth so hard that his jaw ached.

She started to shake her head. "That's not what I—"

"Intended?" he interrupted her again. "Just what did you intend when you were sticking your nose where it didn't belong?"

"I was trying to help."

"No, you were trying to fix my life."

"I wasn't," she began, but she must have thought better of it because she clicked her teeth shut.

He should have stopped there; he realized that. But Julia had started this, and he just couldn't stop the words from coming. "What I don't get is why you go around trying to fix other people when you haven't dealt with your own scars."

Confusion and maybe hurt registered on her face, but he refused to let it get to him. Without giving her time to ask what he was talking about, he turned to Rick and Charity, who were doing a poor job of pretending not to listen, and thanked them for the picnic.

After a quick thanks to Julia, he turned and strode across the parking lot. His hands kept fisting, so he shoved them in his pockets. *That didn't go well.* Julia's words reverberated through his thoughts. She could say that again. And again.

Kyle slid into the driver's seat of his car and closed the door, slamming both hands on the steering wheel. That he shouldn't have come today seemed obvious. He probably shouldn't have climbed out of bed at all. Backing from the parking place, he pulled out of the lot, amazed he didn't pitch gravel as he went.

He couldn't even remember what he and Trooper Lancaster had said to each other as it all flashed back as an angry blur. Worse than whatever they'd said, though it couldn't have been good, was that they'd said it in front of Brett's wife and children. Brett would never forgive him for that just as he would never let him forget that he'd marred the Lancaster name.

While Kyle had awaited his release, all he could think about was moving forward with his family, proving that he'd become a better man. He'd planned to win them all over—Mom, Dad, Jenny, even Brett, though he'd expected a hard-won battle there. But just when he needed more than anything to take a step forward, all he'd done today was to be shoved the proverbial two steps back.

It was all Julia's fault. Or at least part of it was. She'd had no right to invite herself into a situation that she knew nothing about, that was more complicated than she could know.

What had she been thinking, shoving him and his judgmental brother together? Had she believed they would make nice because it was a family picnic? Did she really believe that all the problems could be solved over cold fried chicken and potato salad? How naive was she? His Benedict Arnold stomach betrayed him then by growling and suggesting that home cooking could have solved at least one of *his* problems.

His frustration wasn't even about his wounded pride over how differently he and Julia had envisioned this afternoon's outing. Okay, it did sting to think that while he'd pictured the day like a Monet painting as colorful as "Poppies," she'd imagined a stark intervention. Still, it was more than that. She'd had no right to get involved, even if she'd had good intentions. Didn't she know that a road to a particularly unpleasant place was paved with good intentions?

He and Julia probably had both learned hard lessons today. If she was paying any attention, Julia had learned that she couldn't fix the world, and she had no business trying. He'd learned that allowing himself to believe there might be possibilities for him and Julia Sims would be a mistake.

Kyle trudged up the wide, brick walkway to a massive and impersonal brick Colonial only made more intimidating with the passage of time. At the bottom of the round porch with its mortared design, he hesitated. Maybe it was too soon. Hadn't he made enough mistakes for one day? He'd already further alienated enough relatives this week, even putting off ones he'd just met.

The possibility that he would make a bad situation worse had him delaying a few seconds longer. But hadn't three years been long enough? Hadn't they all wasted enough time, him most of all?

Straightening, Kyle climbed the steps and pushed the doorbell before his fortitude cracked like some of the mortar connecting the bricks beneath his feet. When no one answered, he released the breath he'd been holding. God had His timing, and maybe this just wasn't it.

He pushed the bell a second time for good measure and turned to go, but he heard a click behind the door. Through one of those narrow panes of obscured, colored glass, he saw a distorted view of her before she opened the door.

"Mom." The word sounded as painful as it felt to speak it out loud for the first time in years.

She looked the same, really, though the fine lines on the sides of her mouth had deepened to crevices, and the crinkles at the corners of her eyes had fanned out like sunbursts. It took a few seconds for her to react, her eyes first narrowing then widening. She blinked a few times behind her glasses, as if tapping the memories and recognition back in place.

"Kyle?" If her pain hadn't been clear enough in the gasp that formed his name, then the flood of tears in her eyes brought it into crystalline view.

Without any of the hesitation he'd braced himself

for, Colleen Lancaster's fine-boned arms came around his waist as she stepped outside the door in slipper-clad feet. She buried a mother's sorrow in the center of his chest. His eyes burned and his heart thudded with the need to reach out to the woman he loved more than anyone and had hurt even more. She stood there just holding him, and when she pulled away, his eyes were as damp as hers.

"You came," she said simply.

Kyle stiffened as he stepped back from her, but he forced himself to relax. He'd phoned his parents when he'd been released, had even asked for Brett's number for help with the job, so they knew where he was living. But he had no right to expect them to make the first move in restoring their relationship. The damage was his, and only he could repair it.

"It's so good to see you." He smiled at eyes that were mirrors of his own. "You look beautiful."

She brushed away his comment with a wave of her hand. "Oh, you boys and your flattery." Still, she patted her soft waves of hair that had only become blonder as more strands of silver had settled in alongside the platinum and lemony hues.

"I've missed you so much." As the words left his mouth, he grabbed her for a second hug. Though his mother's shoulder blades protruded more than they had in the past, and she felt thinner than he remembered, Kyle had the first sense of being at home since the prison gates had clicked shut with him on the outside.

"Your father and I…we just couldn't come to see you…there." The last word made a strangled sound in her throat.

"I know." He brushed his hand down her hair that still felt downy soft. "But it's over now."

She stepped back and looked up into his eyes. "Is it?"

With two little words, his mother had asked hundreds of questions about broken laws, broken promises and trust perhaps too shattered to repair. But he had to have hope, and he prayed she hadn't given up hers.

"Yes, it's over. Have a little faith, Mom."

She smiled then, and his heart relaxed.

"Your dad's inside."

Kyle nodded, his insides clutching again. He'd been so caught up in the moment of seeing her that it hadn't struck him as odd that his father hadn't joined her at the front door. With the dealership always closing early on Saturday afternoons, Dad was usually home by this time at night, and he loved visitors.

Colleen pushed the door she'd left partially open and led Kyle in as a guest to the mammoth structure where he'd lived at least half of his life. It still looked the same, like a decorator's showplace where no one was allowed to really live, except in the family room where they'd spent most of their days. He followed her there now, already breathing in the familiar scents of leather and lemon cleaner.

Just where Kyle guessed they might find him, Sam Lancaster dozed in his well-worn brown leather chair, but the man in that chair wasn't the father Kyle had last seen in the courtroom when the jury forewoman had read a guilty verdict. This imposter was but a sliver of that robust, larger-than-life man his father had always been. A wheeled oxygen tank was perched next to the chair and its tube wound up the front of Sam's chest until it disappeared inside his nostrils.

Kyle stopped in the doorway, his hands reaching out to brace himself inside the frame. The room swayed and then returned to stark focus. His father, who'd always been such a light sleeper that Kyle had been forced to invent new ways of sneaking out, didn't even awaken from his nap.

Three years of changes that had touched lightly on Colleen Lancaster looked more like twenty on her husband.

Kyle turned to his mother. "Why didn't you tell me about this?"

"Tell you?" she asked as though he'd posed his question in another language or something.

"Mom, you wrote me nearly every week. Couldn't you have found a few lines to tell me Dad was sick?"

"Sick? Oh, you mean that." She indicated the oxygen tank with a wave of her hand.

"Yes, that. What has he lost? Like, fifty pounds?"

"He has thinned out a bit."

"Mother," he said loudly enough that his father started in his sleep, so he said it again just above a whisper. "Do you really not see what I see?"

"Of course I see it, but none of it is new. Your dad has had mild emphysema for years. Remember, he used to smoke when he was in the Marines? His condition had worsened over time, but he's doing all right."

Come to think of it, Kyle did remember his father having some mild breathing problems. Had he really been so selfish, so focused on his own life, that he'd never realized his father suffered from a serious illness?

"He didn't want me to tell you about it," Colleen admitted. "He's barely facing it himself."

Kyle glanced at his father again now, so frail, the antithesis of the unbendable, if not unbreakable, man he remembered. Of course, it would be tough for Sam Lancaster to face his illness, associating it with weakness. He'd never tolerated weakness well, even in his son.

Those sleeping eyes popped open and their intense stare suggested that at least something about Sam Lancaster hadn't changed.

"What are you two mumbling about? You interrupted a very enjoyable nap." Sam reached up and removed the oxygen tube from his nose.

"Well, you, mister, have napped quite long enough today." Colleen crossed her arms and tapped her foot on the floor. "Now be polite and say hello."

Sam studied his son silently, weighing, measuring, evaluating. Kyle understood when his father looked away that he'd found him lacking. He might have paid his debt to society according to the State of Michigan, but he wasn't even close to repaying what he'd cost his family. Maybe some debts could never be repaid.

Finally, Sam glanced back at Kyle again. "It's good to see you."

"It's good to see you, too," he answered as formally as his father had spoken. He wasn't sure what he'd expected him to say. "Welcome home, son"? Okay, he wouldn't have been upset if that had happened. And he'd read the parable of the Prodigal Son in Luke 15 enough times to hope. *For this son of mine was dead, and has come to life again; he was lost and has been found.* He'd quoted that Scripture so often, wondering how his dad might phrase it.

But he realized now that no matter how elaborately he'd planned this scene between them, it could never have played out the way he'd imagined. He didn't deserve an easy road home, and he would have to face every pothole and detour along the way.

"Are you going to just stand there staring at my sorry state, or are you going to sit down?"

Kyle couldn't help smiling. This was the father he'd known, a curmudgeon who'd always worked hard but who loved harder than he worked. "I guess I can sit awhile."

As if sensing her cue, his mother left the two of them alone. Kyle stepped over to the same pillowy sofa he remembered from years before and sank into its softness.

Sam chuckled but only started coughing hard into his sleeve. It was all Kyle could do to stay in his seat. He didn't even know what to do besides to grab his father and hold him until the wave passed.

When Sam finally got control again, he wiped his eyes. "Now you didn't contradict me, saying there's nothing sorry about the way I look. Should I take offense here?"

"You taught me not to lie."

"That I did."

For a few minutes neither man spoke, each lost in his own heavy thoughts. Finally, Kyle turned back to his father, relying on an easy subject. "How's business going?"

"Economy's been shaky, but people still like to drive new cars. It's always hard to find good help, especially since—"

Sam stopped himself, but Kyle understood that he'd been about to say since Brett had left the family business to work with the state police. Brett had been their father's great hope for taking over the family business.

Twenty minutes before, Kyle would have considered this an opening to tell his father his own plans for the dealership. He would have told him that he'd wasted enough of his life already. But that was twenty minutes ago, before he'd seen his dad. Now he didn't know what to say.

When Kyle glanced up, his father was studying him, as if he already knew that he'd edited his speech. And why.

"Your brother called earlier. Sounds like you've had a busy couple of weeks."

Kyle's throat tightened. Of course, his brother would have told their parents what had happened between them. Twice now. "Not some of my better moments, I'm afraid."

Sam shrugged. "Takes two to battle. You'll have to give your brother some time to come around. He's got a few battle scars that...aren't quite healed."

Kyle nodded, though they weren't talking about his older brother, and both of them knew it. "I have a lot to prove to him. To everyone."

"Takes time." Sam busied his hands reinserting his oxygen tube.

"I've got some of that."

Even as Kyle said it, his own words felt like a punch to the gut. Yes, he probably had some time to try to show everyone he'd hurt that he'd changed, but not everyone had that luxury of time.

Colleen returned to the room then, and Kyle decided to end this first visit. He shook his father's thin hand and kissed his mother's cheek before heading to the door. There would be other visits; he would make sure of it. But Rome had taken a while to build, and he would need to have patience in restoring these relationships, as well.

Still, Kyle didn't have forever to make things right. If that wasn't clear to him before, his father's frail appearance today had announced it in all capital letters and punctuated it with exclamation marks. God never guaranteed anyone a tomorrow. Only today. And today Kyle would focus on his goal because his time to earn absolution from his parents was running out.

Chapter Six

Julia had just completed her bedtime Bible study and was brushing her teeth when her telephone rang. Rushing past the bedside clock that read 10:07, she hurried to the portable phone base in the kitchen. Her pulse raced while questions whirled in her mind. Had something happened to Grace? Was Charity all right? Could anything make this day any worse?

The thought crossed her mind that it might be Kyle calling to give her another piece of his mind, but she dismissed the idea. He would probably just never speak to her again, and she couldn't blame him for it.

It hadn't been her place to restore balance in the Lancaster family tree, and all she'd accomplished was to shake loose a few branches. She understood now that not every broken relationship could be restored in a single conversation, nor could every trespass be easily forgiven.

"Hoolo?" she mumbled into the phone when she reached it on the third ring.

"Julia? Is that you?"

It took her a few seconds to place the voice, and when she did, her pulse tripped again. "Kw…yle?"

Her word came out garbled again, but his chuckle on the other end of the line was as clear as a pin-drop. "Ye…es. Are you brushing your teeth?"

Rather than answer immediately, she leaned over the kitchen sink and spit. "So what if I was?" She turned the water on to a trickle and rinsed the sink.

"You were planning to floss, too, weren't you? It's important not to neglect your gums."

Julia stared at the phone receiver, wondering if this was some strange daydream. "Are you sure this is Kyle?"

"Sure. Oh, you're wondering because I'm not yelling. Sorry." He chuckled again. "It's been a long day, and I'm getting punchy."

"No problem." Her voice managed to sound calm, but she needed something to do with her hands, so she carried the portable phone from room to room, straightening a sofa cover here, fluffing a pillow there.

"I hope you don't mind me calling so late. I wasn't sure if you'd even be home."

This time the chuckle came from her. "It's ten o'clock on a Saturday night. Of course I'm home." She waited for him to react to the joke, but he didn't. Maybe he found self-effacing humor as un-attractive on her as she'd found it on him.

After the silence stretched tight for as long as she could take, Julia spoke up again. "Um, I'm surprised to hear from you. You know, after…"

"You mean, after that scene in the park today. Well, that was hours ago, and it's been a long day and—"

"You said that. Now please, will you be serious because I'm sorry about what I did today. I had no right."

"I'm sorry, too."

Again, she stared at the phone. Not another dressing down, but an apology. This conversation was as strange and confusing as his comment about her family. He'd said she hadn't dealt with her own scars when she didn't have any scars to speak of, and now he was apologizing when it was she who had done something wrong.

"You don't have anything to be sorry about," she said as she sank into her cozy, corduroy sofa.

"If that were only true," he said with a sigh that suggested he regretted events from more than a single day. "I'm sorry I overreacted to your—I don't know—ambush."

"I guess you could call it that."

"Now don't get me wrong. I'm still not pleased with what you did. It was an invasion into my personal life. But you were trying to help, so thank you for that."

"You're thanking me after all that happened this afternoon? It blew up in all our faces."

He laughed out loud then, a melodic baritone sound that filled her ears and made her smile. Calm replaced the anxiety and regret that had tussled inside her since the scene at the park.

"I guess it blew up," he began, "but it must have looked comical with two grown men up in each other's faces like a couple of brawlers."

"No, it made me sad watching a couple of *brothers* who couldn't see the good in each other."

"Oh."

When he didn't say more, Julia wondered if she'd said too much. Had she crossed the line again, daring to invade his personal life when the first time had gone so poorly?

"Anyway," he began again, "I wanted to call to say that I forgive you."

"Thanks." She smiled at the receiver, not bothering to mention that he'd phoned to forgive her rather than waiting for her to phone with another apology.

"I learned a few things through my prison Bible study besides taking personal responsibility for my actions, and one of those lessons is that forgiveness goes two ways," he told her. "You know, that verse from Ephesians 4—*Be kind to one another, tender-hearted, forgiving one another, as God in Christ forgave you.*"

She didn't know what to say. Earlier she hadn't

been able to picture him ever speaking to her again, and he'd been the first to reach out to her. Quoting Scripture, no less.

"I keep surprising you, don't I?"

"Yes, you do."

"Then how about I surprise you some more tomorrow? Would you like to have lunch with me after church?"

Forget tomorrow, he'd surprised her enough right then. After everything that had happened, he still wanted to spend time with her. Part of her couldn't help looking forward to seeing Kyle again, that same disloyal part she'd been battling ever since she'd met him.

She'd better get such romantic notions out of her head for good because after the way she'd invaded his personal life, she was privileged that he still wanted to speak to her at all. If he still thought it possible for them to be friends, then she was downright honored.

"So you'll be at church tomorrow?" she asked.

"You mean, because of Trooper Lancaster? Yeah, I'll be there. My brother will just have to get used to seeing me around." He paused, as if considering that. "I'll have to learn to cross his path without making a scene."

"Sure, let's go to lunch." Somehow she managed not to offer her own two cents about how he should act when he and his brother met next. Their seedling of a new friendship wouldn't allow for unsolicited advice just yet.

"You know what I missed most about this afternoon?" Kyle said. "The chicken. I'd heard all about it, and I didn't even get the chance to taste it."

"I had a piece, but after everything that happened, I had to choke it down. It could have been a pile of sawdust for all I tasted it."

"Was that because you were also eating a slice of humble pie that your sister gave you?"

"What do you mean?"

"She told you that setting us up at the park to mend our fences was a bad idea, didn't she?"

Julia straightened and sat forward on the couch, resting her forearms on her thighs. "How did you know—"

"I have a brother *and* a sister."

"Oh. Right."

So many things about this conversation had been new and pleasant discoveries, but Kyle hadn't answered the one question that still begged for clarification. "Can you tell me something? What changed after you left the park today?"

"I went to see my parents."

"So we'll talk about that at lunch tomorrow?"

"Maybe."

"Whatever you decide."

"Thanks."

Strange, she found she was serious that it didn't

matter whether he told her. It had probably been a difficult visit for him after three years of separation, but it was his situation, not hers, and it was his decision whether or not to share.

They said their good-nights, and Julia carried the phone handset into the bedroom where she usually kept it at night. Though she doubted she would sleep anytime soon, she shut off the light and crawled beneath the sheets. After the fiasco this afternoon, the day could have turned out differently than it had, and she took a moment to thank God for that pleasant end. She was relieved this wouldn't be the last time she spoke to Kyle Lancaster.

Bright sun filtered through the circular stained-glass window behind the pulpit, sending splashes of color on the walls as Kyle entered the Hickory Ridge sanctuary. Funny, he hadn't noticed that window before. The sun might not have been shining just right when he'd come to services or when he'd shown up for work, but he also might have been too preoccupied to notice the window.

That he'd entered by the center aisle instead of by the side door might have had something to do with his new discovery, as well. He skipped the back row this time, taking a seat in the fifth row. Okay, he sat on the opposite side of where he'd seen Brett and his family last Sunday, but it was something.

He tried not to notice Julia, seated on the opposite side of the auditorium next to her sister's family, tried not to see how amazing she looked in a pale yellow, button-up sweater and skirt with flowers all over it. But she drew his attention like a magnet.

Even when he wasn't looking at her, Kyle was still aware of her. Though sometimes he thought he could even feel her gaze on him, every time he glanced sidelong at her, she was studying her Bible or talking with Rick or Charity. The serious-looking woman on Charity's other side had to be Charity's mother, Laura Sims. At least it was a good hint that the woman whispered to Charity but never looked down the aisle toward Julia.

All around Kyle, the pews were filling with church members, many smiling and waving as they took their seats. An attractive older woman with short, dark hair and glasses slid into the pew just down from him.

"Hello, Kyle," she said as she extended her hand. "We haven't met. I'm Mary Nelson."

Kyle shook her hand and returned her friendly smile. He didn't have to wonder how she knew who he was: if she hadn't heard about his prayer meeting dinner spectacle, she could have seen his picture in this week's bulletin. What he couldn't figure out was why Mary's name sounded familiar to him. The cute little blond girl who bounced into the pew on Mary's other side didn't answer his question, though the child's face was familiar, too.

"Hi, Grandma Mary," the child said, and then she wrapped her little arms around her in a tight hug.

Mary pulled away to arm's length from the child and smiled over at Kyle. "This sweetie is Rebecca."

"Mommy said I could sit with you if you say it's okay."

"It's fine. Are you getting excited about the new baby? I just know you'll be a great big sister."

Of course. Kyle had seen Rebecca's picture on Reverend Bob's desk. She was his granddaughter, and the woman the child had called "grandma" was the minister's "lady friend," as Andrew had referred to her.

Sure enough, Mary glanced up a few rows and waved to Hannah McBride, who was seated with a blond man Kyle assumed was her husband, Todd.

"We're so pleased to have you here at Hickory Ridge," Mary whispered as the organ processional began, and the church's two ministers took their seats on the opposite sides of the podium.

"Thanks," he whispered back.

During the opening hymn, an enthusiastic singing of "How Great Thou Art," Kyle glanced back at the woman Andrew had described as a blessing to Reverend Bob's life. She'd certainly made Kyle feel welcome. According to Andrew, Mary had been good for Reverend Bob after his last scandalous relationship with a woman who'd used their friendship to embezzle money from the church.

When Reverend Bob stepped to the lectern a few minutes later, he scanned the congregation, smiling when his gaze paused on Mary. The warmth in the minister's expression had Kyle sneaking another peek at Julia, but this time she was looking at him. She gave a tiny wave before facing the front of the church again.

"During his ministry on earth, Jesus taught his followers many things, and forgiveness was among the most critical," Reverend Bob said. "In Luke 15, Jesus spoke about the kind of forgiveness that God offers His children, told through a story about a man who forgave his son."

The Prodigal Son. Kyle's fingers automatically moved to the Book of Luke in his Bible. He wondered if Reverend Bob had been planning this sermon for a while or if he'd decided to speak on it in honor of his newest employee.

"Did the man turn his son away though he'd blown his inheritance on booze and women?" Reverend Bob paused for effect, as if the congregation didn't already know how this story ended. "No. He welcomed his son home with open arms. Our Father in Heaven is like that. He's always waiting for us with open arms when we finally return to Him."

Kyle couldn't help smiling at that. He for one was grateful that God had continued to wait for him while he'd stumbled through the darkness, not looking for the light but finding it anyway.

"Was everyone happy about the Prodigal's return?" The minister shook his head. "Not everyone. His brother questioned their father's easy acceptance of his wayward son and was upset about the party given in his honor."

Kyle's thoughts immediately went to another brother, someone who seemed just as unhappy as the man in the parable about his brother's return. Across the aisle, Brett sat next to Tricia with their two older children. Kyle glanced away, not sure if his brother had noticed him.

Brett hadn't wanted him to come back. Kyle had always suspected it, but having it laid out there before him cut him deeply. Maybe Brett didn't trust that he'd returned as a changed man. Or maybe he believed Kyle had already used up all his second chances.

If Kyle's first guess were true, he would have to prove Trooper Lancaster wrong. By sticking around, he could demonstrate that the changes in him were neither contrived nor fleeting. Regarding second chances, there was nothing he could do except to work hard and hope Brett would change his mind about him.

"So if Jesus used one of His great lessons to show us the importance of a father accepting his son back with open arms, how do you think God wants us to treat our brothers and sisters when they return to the church?" Reverend Bob asked as he ended his sermon.

Kyle looked to the front of the church, expecting the minister to be staring straight at him. Reverend Bob was scanning the whole congregation, but Kyle still figured there might as well have been a target on his forehead as clearly as the sermon was directed his way.

Even before today's sermon, the members of Hickory Ridge had gotten the message about welcoming others back into the Christian community. Several members had gone out of their way to make him feel at home. One in particular had gone beyond that basic call of duty, even if her plans to help had left a trail of destruction in their wake.

He glanced sidelong at Julia, this time catching her watching him. Her gaze met his for a fraction of a second, and then she looked away, a secret smile playing on her lips. Of course, she would have made the connection between him and Reverend Bob's sermon.

Kyle almost smiled himself. He still didn't think she should have thrown him and his brother together, but he had to give her credit for trying. She was proof herself that damaged family relationships could be mended, and her belief that he and Brett could work out their problems was contagious. She gave him a reason to hope.

Chapter Seven

Julia slid into the vinyl-covered booth at Leo's Coney Island and then tried to untangle her skirt that refused to scoot with her. Kyle was grinning when she looked up after righting it.

Instead of commenting, he glanced around the restaurant, taking in the rows of packed tables and booths. "This place does a good Sunday business."

"You should see the Big Boy on Milford Road. That's where our church crowd usually hangs out." She paused to take a sip from her water glass. "We usually slide a bunch of tables together and eat and laugh for a couple of hours. By the time we're done, it's usually almost time for the evening worship service."

Kyle lifted an eyebrow as he studied her, but he didn't say anything.

Julia's cheeks burned. "Oh, you probably wonder

why I suggested that we come here instead of going to the place where the rest of the congregation would be."

"I was kind of wondering."

"I wanted it to be just the two of us…so I could apologize again."

He shook his head. "You already apologized. Anyway, it was nothing."

"If it was nothing, I'd sure hate to see how you react when something big happens."

"Okay, I deserved that."

"Why don't we just forget about yesterday?" she said. "It wasn't one of my better moments."

"You mean, you can top that one?"

His incredulous expression had her chuckling. "You know, I'm not sure I can."

"Whew." He brushed back the hair off his forehead in relief. "I was worried."

"So we can forget about it?"

"I'm willing." Kyle pulled two laminated menus from behind the napkin container and slid one her way. "I guess we'll have to ask Tricia's kids to forget it, too."

"Oh, yeah, I forgot they were there." Julia frowned. "I doubt they'll forget it anytime soon. I'll tell Tricia to send the counseling bill my way when Lani, Rusty Jr. and Max realize how much my picnic damaged them."

"What about the baby...Anna?" He winked. "No therapist for her? Won't she feel deprived?"

"I was hoping that someone her age might forget she saw anything at all."

He made a wrong-answer sound in his throat, but then he chuckled. "Maybe they'll all forget. Eventually."

Picking up his menu off the table, he scanned the photographs. "So what's good here?"

"Probably a lot of things, but the place is known for its Coney dogs."

"With chili sauce, onions and mustard?"

"That's the only way."

"It's been a long time since I've eaten one of those."

Julia returned his smile, wondering just how often he could say that about restaurants' specialties or even home-cooked meals. He probably missed a lot of things during his time behind bars.

When the waitress arrived with her prim apron and tiny notepad, they both ordered the same thing: a couple of Coneys—loaded—and fries. After his plate was set in front of him, Kyle leaned down to inhale the aroma, but instead of digging right in, he bowed his head for a silent prayer of thanks.

He had to have recognized Julia's surprise when he opened his eyes, but he only lifted the Coney off his plate and took a big bite. When was she going to stop being surprised every time Kyle did or said something that demonstrated his commitment to his faith? She had no business judging another person's heart. She needed to stay focused on her own relationship with God.

Oblivious to her private lecture, Kyle chewed his food, swallowed and then closed his eyes again. "Oh, I remember thcsc."

"You mean, the heartburn?"

His eyes flicked open. "Let me enjoy this, will you?"

"All right." She took a bite of her hot dog and licked her lips.

They ate without speaking, the only sounds around them the clinking of forks on the white porcelain dishes. Julia didn't find the silence between them uncomfortable, though. Just the opposite, in fact. When twenty-four hours before she'd wondered if Kyle would ever speak to her again, here they were together, *not speaking to each other,* and she for one felt content.

Maybe they could still be friends after all. Already, they were back to their friendly banter, and it didn't even involve self-deprecating humor.

"You know the only problem with this stuff," Kyle began, waiting for her to look across the table again. "It disappears too fast."

Julia glanced at his plate without even a drip of chili on it and then back at her own where she still had one hot dog, piled high with its messy sauce, and a pile of fries. She pushed her plate his way.

"You sure?"

She nodded. There was something nice and bonding about sharing her food with him, especially when he seemed to enjoy it so much. Sharing with him served as further proof that a friendship between them was still possible, despite everything.

Julia reached for a few of the fries, but she ate slowly, hoping to delay finishing the meal. They were having such a nice time that she didn't want it to end. But Kyle inhaled the rest of her lunch as efficiently as he'd consumed his own, and he sat there watching her chew her last bite.

As soon as she finished, he snapped up the check, dropped a few dollars' tip on the table and headed toward the cash register near the exit. She had no choice but to follow, wishing there were something clever she could say to make him want to stay.

At the door, he turned back to her. "It's so nice out. Let's take a walk. I need to stretch my legs and work off a few Coneys."

"Sounds good." It sounded better than that, but she didn't want to startle him by jumping too enthusiastically at his offer.

Instead of heading to the lot behind the plaza where they'd parked their cars, they turned right on Main Street, following the sidewalk to the center of downtown.

As soon as they'd crossed Commerce Road, Julia turned back to him. "A lot of places are closed on

Sundays." Even the few that were open probably weren't having a strong Sunday business, she figured, as dead as downtown appeared to be. A few cars passed through downtown, probably on their way to either Michigan 59 or Interstate 96.

"Doesn't matter if the stores are closed," he said. "We can window-shop."

"My favorite kind of shopping. On a teacher's salary, I don't get a lot of chances for the other kind."

"I'm a little out of practice myself."

They passed a few of the quaint shops, one selling Native American jewelry and another women's and children's clothes. The *Milford Times* office was a little farther up on the right. Kyle stopped there, studying the current display behind the window.

"Ever seen one of these?" Julia pointed to the recent articles and local real estate listings. "Not many newspaper offices have their own storefronts."

"Welcome to life in a small town."

"Milford sure is one of those. Everybody knows everyone else, and for those we don't know personally, we sure know *about* them."

"That sure makes a guy like me uncomfortable."

Julia glanced sidelong at him and caught him watching her. She smiled. Okay, he was targeting himself in his humor, but it wasn't as biting as it had been before.

"Uncomfortable, huh? Feel like you're being watched at church?" She shook her head. "I wouldn't worry about that. Our members know a few things about you, but I thought they were doing a good job of making you feel welcome. Well… except for Brett."

"And that lady who was sitting with your family at church. Was that Charity's mom?"

She nodded. "Laura Sims." She took a few steps away from him and then stopped and turned back. "Did she say something to you?"

"To me? Not really." Turning away from the newspaper office, he caught up to her in three long strides. "But she had a few things to say *about* me, all within my hearing distance. Apparently she doesn't think the prison ministry or my involvement in it are good ideas."

"She doesn't agree with a lot of things. Or people."

"You're one of them, aren't you? You said she doesn't come to events when she knows you're invited."

"Can't blame her, really."

Kyle stopped walking, turning his head to study her. "Can't blame her?"

"How would you like someone to be around who always reminded you of the worst thing you'd ever done?"

The side of his mouth lifted, but he didn't say

anything. Of course, he knew what that was like. He'd lived it a lot lately.

"Anyway, I'm proof that Mrs. Sims presented herself as a widow when her husband was very much alive and an *ex*-husband with a new wife and another child."

Kyle shrugged, making a distasteful expression. "So, then it's her punishment to see you just like…" He let his words trail away, but it was clear he wondered whether being near his brother was *his* punishment.

"I don't want to be anybody's punishment. Charity's my sister, and Mrs. Sims is her mother. We can't help but be tied to each other. I just wish we could be friends."

"You do have an interesting taste in friends. Present company excluded, of course."

"Of course."

Kyle turned to her again, his eyebrows drawn together. "Let me get this straight. Someone with a checkered past conveniently forgets her own sins and serves as the moral compass for the church community?"

"She's all right." Julia felt guilty for the times when the same question had crossed her mind. She'd prayed a lot to feel charitable where Mrs. Sims was concerned.

"She just needs some compassion. Mrs. Sims has tried to heal her relationship with Charity, but she still tends to measure everyone else by impossible standards. I wonder if she's so judgmental because she's hurting inside."

In front of a jewelry store, Kyle stopped and turned to face her. "You know what I think? I think Laura Sims is lucky to have someone like you trying to be her friend."

Julia's face warmed, as she couldn't help being pleased by his praise, no matter how undeserved. She would have told him at least the second part, but he spoke again before she had the chance.

"A lot of people should count their blessings that you've chosen to be their friend."

She swallowed. How was she supposed to answer that without making his statement even more personal than it already was? She'd never expected him to speak to her again, and now he was thanking her for her friendship. She was the one who'd been blessed.

"Thanks," she managed to say.

"Hey, is there any place around here to sit?" Kyle asked, glancing farther down Main Street.

"I thought you needed to stretch and work off the hot dogs." She was surprised how easily she transitioned from that awkward moment to their easy banter.

"It was too much jostling for the dogs." With a grimace, he pressed his fist against his chest, hinting that the predicted heartburn had struck after all.

She pointed toward the area between two buildings on the west side of the street. "Follow me."

"Just walk slowly, okay?" But he was laughing as he said it, so he couldn't have been too miserable.

Crossing by one of those midstreet crosswalks that pedestrians used at their own risk, she led him to the bricked area where a defunct fountain stood close to the road. Farther back was the same gleaming white gazebo Julia had passed many times before.

Julia climbed the steps on the one open side, taking a seat on the bench next to the entrance. She'd had a daydream or two about this gazebo, of a sweet embrace with some yet unnamed hero, but strangely, she'd never pictured it as a place for respite for the under-the-weather.

She was still grinning over that thought when Kyle entered behind her. "Enjoying my misery?"

"No, I was just thinking of a story."

"Care to share?"

She shook her head.

"Your choice," he said with a shrug.

He looked out the side of the gazebo that faced the parking lot and then settled on the bench opposite Julia. For a fleeting second, she wished he'd sat next to her instead, but then she tucked the errant thought away where it belonged.

"Feeling any better yet?"

Kyle hit his fist on his chest twice, as if to check. "Good as new."

"Good to hear. I'm sure Reverend Bob would be bothered if I took you out to lunch and killed you off before the evening service."

"Not good for church outreach."

He chuckled, and she joined him, but he straightened, becoming serious.

"I thought about that last night." His eyes took on a faraway look as he watched a few cars travel past them on the street ahead.

She waited a few seconds, hoping he would clarify, but when she couldn't wait any longer she asked, "That I would kill you off?"

With a start, he glanced back at her. "What? Oh. No." He shook his head as if to clear his thoughts. "When I was with my father last night, I thought that he might not be around long enough for me to prove to him that I can make something of myself."

She couldn't quite see how he'd made that intellectual leap from her joke about killing him off to the loss of his father, but she could tell it had been pressing on his thoughts. She understood intimately how painful the loss of a parent could be. "I'm sorry. I hadn't heard your dad was gravely ill."

"Not gravely ill. But he's definitely frail. Mom said it's been a slow decline. I would have known that if I'd been there to see it for myself."

Kyle's frustration that he hadn't been was written plainly on his face.

"There was nothing you could have done, even if you knew."

"I guess that's true," he answered on a sigh.

Standing, he stepped to the gazebo entrance and leaned against the rail. For a long time, he didn't speak but stared out at the street.

Last night she'd told him he could decide whether to share what had happened at his parents' house, and she was trying not to pry. He had the right to his privacy, and he'd already told her this much, so she needed to be satisfied. He'd accused her of being someone who tried to fix people, and she didn't want to prove him right.

"I don't know what I expected when I went over there," he began, without looking her way. "That I would be welcomed back with open arms or something? Or that I would be given the keys to the city."

"That whole prodigal thing."

When he turned back to her, he lifted a shoulder and let it drop. "So you were listening at church?"

"I figured that sermon might have hit close to home for you."

"So you thought I was the target of Reverend Bob's message, too?"

"You weren't alone. Brett probably felt like he was on the hot seat, too." She chuckled before becoming serious again. "You know, all of us need reminders that God is always there, waiting to forgive us. I think that message was meant to speak to us all."

He seemed to consider her observation and then nodded. "Anyway, as far as the Scripture story goes, Mom did welcome me back with open arms. Right into her arms."

"And your dad?" Okay, she'd tried to hold back, to let him tell her in his own time, but *his time* ran in slow motion, and she was dying for answers.

"He didn't throw me out, anyway. He didn't— maybe couldn't—get up from the chair at all."

Emotion lodged in her throat as she imagined how it must have felt for Kyle, seeing his father that way after such a long separation. She'd only seen Sam Lancaster in TV commercials, and even she couldn't picture him looking anything less than sassy and healthy.

"But he spoke to you, right?" She waited for his nod before she continued. "And he didn't say this was the last time he would speak to you?"

"No, he didn't say that. Said something about it taking time to heal."

"Sounds like a smart man to me."

"He's that, all right."

He didn't say any more, and she suspected he wouldn't. She wasn't disappointed, though. Kyle had opened up to her more than she'd ever expected. More amazing than that, she might even have helped him find some perspective on what he'd told her.

She didn't know how this new revelation regarding his father's health would affect his grand plan of taking over the family business, but she sensed that something had changed. She didn't ask him what. He would tell her if and when he was ready.

She waited in case he had more to say, but the only sound she heard was a siren in the distance. The wind had picked up and was pulling at the strands of her hair that had fallen free from her knot.

Finally, Kyle looked over at her. When their gazes connected, he gestured with a move of his head in an unspoken question about whether she was ready to leave. She stood to let him know that she was. They descended the steps and continued across the bricked area.

"I'm glad we did this," he said once they were back on the sidewalk where they could see the storefronts again.

"Me, too."

"Even if I'll be chewing on antacids all day."

She turned to find him grinning. They both knew that their detour had much more to do with unsettled thoughts than upset stomachs.

On the way back to their cars, they discussed the evening service, which Julia was pleased to learn Kyle would be attending. They wouldn't have much time until the service, either, she discovered as soon as she opened her car door and the digital clock showed it was already after four o'clock. She'd turned her cell phone off at church and had forgotten to turn it back on, so the late hour surprised her. They'd spent much of the afternoon talking, and it hadn't seemed like any time at all.

With a wave, she drove away, feeling content. She couldn't believe the contrast between their parting words today and those at the park on Saturday. What a difference a day made.

Not only had Kyle forgiven her, but also when he'd needed someone to talk to, he'd chosen her. She was so honored that he'd put his trust in her; she didn't deserve it. She probably didn't deserve his friendship, either, but he seemed to be offering that, as well. She planned to work hard at being Kyle Lancaster's friend.

Chapter Eight

Kyle parked in the circular drive outside Johnson Elementary School, leaving his car windows down to keep the car as cool as possible on the hottest day in May so far. The lot next to the building was nearly empty except for a few straggling cars, probably belonging to teachers and custodial staff. Because the sign on the front door directed visitors to check in at the main office, he stopped by there first, but even those staff members had packed up for the day.

An older gentleman with a school employee badge that said, "Ken Samuels, Custodial Staff," stopped him in the hallway.

"May I help you, sir?" From his hand dangled a set of keys with which he was probably getting ready to lock the front door that Kyle had just entered.

"I'm looking for Miss Sims. Is she still in the building?"

"If anybody's still here late on the Thursday before Memorial Day, Miss Sims would be a likely candidate." The man chuckled. "Here, let me take you." He took a few steps away, but then he stopped and looked back at Kyle suspiciously. "Are you a parent? The kids don't have school tomorrow."

Kyle shook his head at the first suggestion, not bothering to try to respond to the other comments. "Ah, no. Not a parent."

The older man cocked his head to the side. "Then why would you be visiting one of our first-grade classrooms?"

"I'm Kyle Lancaster from Hickory Ridge Church. Julia was supposed to meet me at my office an hour ago, but she didn't show, so I thought she might still be at work."

The man relaxed, tucking his thumbs through his belt loops. "Good guess. I'd say Julia's here late a few afternoons a week, mostly giving extra help to students."

Julia hadn't mentioned that about herself, but Kyle didn't have a hard time imagining it. Not long ago, he'd accused her of trying to *fix* people, but he realized now that it was too simplistic an answer when it came to figuring out Julia Sims. From the occasional glimpses he'd seen of her over the past two weeks, he would say now that helping people was as innate to Julia's personality as her belief that there was good in all people. He, for one, was glad she believed that.

"I don't know for sure if she's in there, but her classroom is down that hall." The man pointed down a dimly lit hallway. "Last room on the left."

Kyle thanked the man, and they headed in opposite directions. Obviously the Milford rumor mill hadn't done its job effectively if the custodian hadn't recognized him by his name. Good thing. He probably wouldn't have let him anywhere near Julia's classroom if he knew who he was.

Inside the room, Julia sat at a desk, her attention on a book laying open in front of her, her lips pressed into a grim line. Though the rest of her remained still, with her left hand, she tapped a pencil on her desk in a furious pace. He was surprised by the temptation to cross the room and smooth her furrowed brow with his thumb. He didn't like whatever made her so sad.

"That must be some serious reading."

Julia's head jerked, and her pencil fell to the floor, rolling under the desk.

"I didn't know you were there," she said, stating the obvious. Her head disappeared under the desk as she bent to retrieve her pencil.

"And I didn't know you were left-handed."

She popped back up from beneath the desk. "Most creative people are."

"I guess I wouldn't know about that." He waved his dominant hand: the right one.

By the time she was seated in her desk chair again, he had pulled a plastic-backed student chair up and had lowered himself into it. *Folded* was a better word. Like a piece of origami, with his knees close to his chin.

"What are you doing here, any—" She stopped herself, peeking at the wall clock. "Oh. Sorry. I didn't realize it was so late. I was just reading— Forget it."

"No big deal. I figured you'd forgotten, and I hadn't seen the location where all this great education takes place, so I stopped by."

"How'd you get in the building, anyway?"

"The custodian met me near the front office."

"I'm surprised Ken didn't send you packing."

"He let me stay after I asked for you and told him I work at Hickory Ridge."

Julia gave him a meaningful look that suggested she understood how unsettling that had been for him. He'd been accepted because of one association when he been rejected because of another.

"I was working with a student, and then I started studying my reference book, and I lost track of time."

"Can't blame you. If I had reading material as fascinating as that, I would never leave the house." He pointed to the book that had fallen closed on her desk. *Reading Strategies That Promise Success*.

Shaking her head, she stared down at the book. "It's just that nothing I've tried so far is working. Text to text. Experience to text. Max just isn't making the associations yet."

"Max? As in Brett and Tricia's son, Max?"

Startling, Julia looked up at him. "Oh, I can't believe I said his name."

"I won't repeat anything."

"I still shouldn't have brought it up." Pushing out her bottom lip, she blew a frustrated breath that lifted some of her bangs. "He was just in here, and we were trying a few new things. He tries so hard. I know it just has to come at a teachable moment, but—"

"Are you worried about dyslexia?"

Julia shook her head hard, as if to push away the thought. "It's too soon to be jumping to any kind of conclusions. But learning is a tough enough job for children without them having to face extra obstacles."

"You never know. He might still catch on."

"I'm praying he does." She patted the book, as if its contents might also hold part of the key.

"You must be a great teacher. I wish I'd had a few who were as dedicated as you when I was growing up."

"I'm a good teacher, but look how bad a volunteer I am. I totally blew off our meeting."

"Not totally. That's the beauty of doing our research on the Internet. These searches don't have to happen during regular business hours."

"What are you suggesting?"

"How about we grab some takeout and go back to work in my office?"

"Will you be paid overtime for this?"

"Overtime? Are you kidding? Do you know how hard the Finance committee had to work to even find money to pay me a salary?"

"Right." She straightened her desk, placing the book she'd been studying in a satchel along with a stack of papers and her grade book. "And you still want to work several more hours at the office?

"Beats another night at home watching the Tigers lose."

"Okay. Be prepared, though. Traffic will be bad on Main Street because everyone's trying to get to their cottages up north for Memorial Day weekend."

"Forecasters are calling for a beautiful weekend. Just like summer." He studied her for a few seconds. "Why aren't you leaving town today like everybody else?"

"First, I don't have a cottage up north, and second, I have to work tomorrow. It's not a day off for teachers. Just students. We have an in-service."

"Glad to hear I'm not the only one working tomorrow. I even have a meeting."

She stood and was hefting the satchel onto her shoulder, but she stopped and lowered the bag to the desk. "Does this mean there's finally some movement on the new ministry?"

Instead of leaving, which had likely been her plan, she crossed to the classroom's Dry Erase board and started wiping it down. Though he recognized her attempt to get him to talk, he played along anyway.

"Some progress. Reverend Bob, Andrew and I will be meeting with leaders from the ecumenical council. So far the local ministers seem to be on board, but we'll see when everybody has to put their money where their mouths are."

She looked back from the board. "But you said our church is already funding your position for the next…" She waited for him to fill in the blank.

"Twelve months."

Having unfolded his body from his cramped seat and used the edge of the desk to pull himself to standing, Kyle moved to the other end of the Dry Erase board and started wiping the last tiny smudges with an eraser.

He didn't bother reminding Julia that he'd never planned to stick with the position at the church long enough to use up the year's worth of funding. That was well-traveled territory, and his grand plan had hit a few major potholes already.

"If you have funding, then why do you need the other churches to commit?"

"My salary is just part of the ministry expense. We'll need funds for new Bibles, Bible study materials and office supplies. Travel will be another major expense." He paused, thinking of other obvious needs. "We'll need help from the other churches to make this thing work."

Julia was grinning when he looked to the other end of the board. "Sounds as if you're more invested in this project than you expected you would be."

"Just doing my job," he said with a shrug. "I've already talked with the warden at 'Club Jackson'—that's Jackson State Prison. But I don't know whether we'll be able to visit there or not since it's the intake center for all new guests of the state penal system before they're sent to more permanent facilities, and the inmates are in isolation twenty-three hours a day."

Julia was quiet as she put her eraser in the magnetic holder in the middle of the board and then as she took his eraser and put it away, as well. When she was finished, she turned back to him.

"Can you imagine how lonely and frightening it has to be for the people in there?"

The compassion in her eyes made emotion clog his throat. He coughed into his hand to clear it. "I don't have to imagine. I remember."

She cleared her own throat and smiled. "That's why you're the perfect man to guide this new ministry. You can relate to these people in a way that no one else could."

"Maybe," was all he said. Sure, this ministry plan

with an ex-con as a consultant seemed like a great idea on paper. Kyle understood the boredom of prison life, the daily ritual of schedules, the struggle for dominance in a society so different from anything experienced on the outside. Yes, he would be able to relate to inmates on those areas. But he had yet to step inside a prison wall since his release. How could he bear that deafening mechanical click of a cell lock again without losing his mind?

As if she recognized that the conversation needed to end there, Julia crossed to the storage closet near the door and retrieved her purse. "Do you have plans for the rest of the holiday weekend?"

Kyle stepped back to her desk. "Why do you ask? You're not suggesting another family picnic with surprise guests, are you?"

"No, I learned my lesson there." She paused, shaking her head. "Anyway, a group from church will be going out all over Milford on Saturday, doing maintenance and repair work at the homes of local senior citizens."

"Oh, yeah. Andrew mentioned something about it last week, but I'd forgotten about it."

"Can we count you in?"

"Sure, I'd love to help." Having more time to spend with Julia had its appeal as well, but he didn't mention that.

Kyle reached for the strap of Julia's bag, and after an unspoken request for permission, shouldered it for her. With one last look back to make sure everything was orderly, she switched off the lights.

Outside the darkened room in the barely brighter hallway, the custodian Kyle had met earlier was unwinding a vacuum cleaner cord, a process that took an inordinate amount of time. The man might have led Kyle to Julia's classroom, but he was still checking up on him.

"Hey, Ken," Julia called over to him. "Getting ready to close up for the night?"

"Almost. No rush anyway. It's going to be a while before traffic clears."

She took a few steps away from him and then turned back. "Oh. Thanks for letting Kyle come to my classroom. I can't believe I forgot our meeting, earlier."

"Seemed like a nice enough young man. You need one of those to come around more often."

Julia's cheeks were red as she hurried toward the exit. Once they were outside the door, she turned and pulled on the handle to make sure it had locked.

"You'll have to forgive Ken. Ever since I got this job, he's been a father figure to me, and he's always trying to play match—" She stopped herself and covered her eyes with the back of her hand.

"Why do you keep apologizing for people who try set you up? It has to be great having so many people who care enough about you to want you to be happy."

"It's okay, I guess." But when she lowered her hand, she frowned. "Why can't everybody realize that I'm already happy? I'm just fine. I have a job I love and one that allows me to support myself. I own my own house. Well, the bank and I own it. I have friends and family who support me. Why can't that be enough?"

She'd just listed with surety all of the things he worried about in his own life, but this wasn't about him. "They just want the best for you. And Ken couldn't possibly have known that you and I are just friends. He couldn't have known about us working together on the Homecoming or anything."

He supplied enough excuses to make her feel better, but her frustration still puzzled him. She hadn't been bothered when Hannah had tried to set them up a few weeks ago. She'd even told him about some of her matchup horror stories. What was different about today? As he'd said, the custodian couldn't have known why they were meeting. Or that they were just friends.

Were they? The question whirled through his thoughts. Would he spend this much time thinking about a woman who was *just a friend?* Would he wonder so many times a day what Julia would think of his conversation with the warden or if the story Andrew told him that afternoon would make her smile?

A thought struck him then, but it was so unlikely

that he almost dismissed it. Julia was probably only bothered by the custodian's assumption because she'd worked hard to rebuild their friendship after the picnic incident, but Kyle couldn't help wondering if it was something more. Could it be possible that Julia was having a hard time remembering that they were just friends? He could sympathize. Whether he realized she deserved someone better or not, he was having a pretty hard time remembering it himself.

"How could people simply disappear into thin air?"

Kyle looked so frustrated as he sat at his desk, his elbows planted on top and his chin resting in the *V* formed by his palms, that it was all Julia could do not to reach across the desk and ruffle his hair. She doubted the gesture would go over well.

"They haven't disappeared. They just haven't realized how hard they've made it for us to find them."

She glanced at the paper that still contained a list of about sixty families neither of them had yet to locate. Some had common surnames. Others hadn't provided any forwarding address.

Kyle stared down at the same list. "I can't believe there are still this many missing families."

"Well, look at all the ones we've located." She indicated the pile of foil-lined invitations they'd already made out to another forty families. "And look at these great invitations. We are so blessed to have the owners of a stationery store among our members. They donated all of these at their cost."

She reached over to touch the stack of parchment-style envelopes but stopped before her fingers could brush the paper. Already Kyle had pushed the envelopes to the far side of the desk to avoid having them stained by their carryout spread. Sandwiches, fries and sweating soft drinks wouldn't make great decorations on their invitations. With a few weeks remaining until they would post them, they wanted to avoid staining them.

"Yeah, they're nice," Kyle said finally.

Still, when he turned back to his computer, he was frowning again. She could relate to his frustration. Even with the two of them searching individually, they'd only located less than half of the remaining former members. Tonight, though they'd been working for hours, they hadn't added even one more name to the list.

"Forty," he said as he tapped the keys, pulling up a screen to do yet another computer search.

"I know." Julia realized their work tonight would probably have gone faster if she'd been at the keys because she was a more seasoned Internet user, but she tried to be patient. They probably wouldn't have made any new discoveries anyway. Each road led to another dead end.

"It's amazing that there could be this many families who have left the church." Kyle pointed first to the pile of invitations and then to the list of those yet to be located. "Isn't that about half of the whole church membership?"

She nodded. "This is a transient area, and Hickory Ridge has been around for a long time. People come and go because of jobs or other life changes. Some of our friends we only have for a season, while others become more permanent fixtures here."

He seemed to mull that over and then turned back to the computer, his fingers perched above the keys. "Any new ideas about how to find the missing ones?"

"Your guess is as good as mine." She reached into the container of cold French fries, using one to smear the puddle of remaining ketchup inside the carryout container, but she didn't bother putting the food in her mouth.

"Now you're absolutely sure they want to be found?"

"Not *absolutely* sure," she began, and then looked up at him, narrowing her gaze. "That's the second time you've mentioned them maybe not wanting to be found. Do you know something that I don't?"

He shook his head. "Not really. I just know that sometimes people in this world would prefer to disappear rather than to face up to the things they've done. And sometimes they're better off staying gone."

Julia studied him, his words not making sense. "We're not talking about you, are we?"

"I'm right here, aren't I? I might have wished sometimes that I could disappear, but I decided to stick it out instead."

"Then who are we talking about?"

Kyle stared into her eyes, searching for something—she didn't know what. When she was convinced he would tell her whatever was hanging heavy in his thoughts, he lowered his gaze to his desk and then turned his head to look out the window. Whatever he might have shared with her, whatever trust he might have placed in her, was gone.

"Okay," he said, "there has to be something else we can try."

Julia grabbed a pen and the notebook she'd been doodling on earlier. She was running out of ideas. "With the auto industry as volatile as it's been the last few years, some of these families have moved more than once by now, maybe to different states. There have probably been some divorces, some marriages, a few deaths."

Kyle had been rubbing his temples with his eyes closed, but his lids flicked open. "The best source of our information might not be the Internet at all."

"What do you mean?"

"You know how news travels in churches?" He

waited for her nod before he continued. "Well, church members are great sources of information about their old friends. If we post this list in the church bulletin, I know somebody's going to be able to give us some leads. The other members probably don't even realize they have information that might help."

"That's a great idea. I'll ask Andrew to put it in this Sunday's bulletin."

She stared at the notebook in her hands, the doodled circles and three-dimensional boxes offering no additional suggestions. But something Kyle had said pulled at the strings of her memory. She didn't know anything, did she? She hadn't been around Hickory Ridge nearly as long as Charity or any of the other members. She didn't have nearly enough history to remember....

"Wait. Darcy." She looked down at the list of names again. *Darcy Boyd* was near the top of the list. The young mother had left Milford two years before with her twin sons after a messy divorce. Julia was aware that Darcy had returned to Iowa to be near her parents, but when Julia had searched for her, she'd looked only under the woman's married name. She'd considered that Darcy might have taken her maiden name back, but Julia hadn't been able to recall it. Until now.

"Do a search for Darcy Quinlin in Iowa. Muscatine, I think."

As if he recognized that a breakthrough might be at hand, Kyle asked no questions but started typing instead, following the same steps she'd been repeating the last few weeks. In the White Pages' listing, some promising information appeared on the screen: Quinlin, D.

"That's it!"

"You're sure?" He turned back from the screen to look at her.

"Sure enough to place a quick phone call." She pulled her cell phone from her purse and started dialing.

"Okay then, that's fifty-nine families to go."

She frowned as she waited for the line to ring. "Way to rain on my parade."

"Well, if someone in the church knows a little detail about each of these families, we might be able to clear this list in nothing flat."

"That's better."

Kyle smiled at her, and for a few seconds, she forgot all about committees and projects. It was great just being here with him, even if they were fighting all the wrong turns of the information superhighway together.

While they were hunting for information on the remaining fifty-nine families, she would have the opportunity to spend more time with him. She wasn't in any hurry to locate the last one.

Chapter Nine

Julia propped the ladder against the modest white two-story and started up the shaking steps, her hands gripping the side rails as tightly as she could. She tried not to think about what might happen if she took one misstep or leaned too far one way or the other.

This wasn't the job she would have chosen. Couldn't she have pulled the work assignment for something a little easier, like window washing on the first level?

With each step higher, her insides tightened. Maybe she should have mentioned a slight fear of heights before she agreed to help clear the blocked gutters at Mrs. Burreski's house. And, as sweaty as her hands were becoming, she could hardly call it *slight*.

Suddenly the ladder beneath her feet stilled, causing one of her shoes to slip from its rung. She hugged the ladder in a death grip until she could secure her footing again.

"Hey, are you okay up there?" Kyle called from below.

Risking death and dismemberment, she tilted her head so she could see him below her. He stood there, looking strong and steady.

"I'm fine. Why do you ask?" Her voice cracked only a little, which she considered an accomplishment.

"I don't know. Because you're climbing that thing like you're being forced to walk the plank."

"I have no idea what you're talking about."

"Okay, then. If you're fine, I'll go help the guys fixing that leaky faucet in the kitchen. I wonder how many volunteers it takes to replace a leaky valve."

"All right." She took another step higher, but Kyle must have released the ladder because it started shaking again. She hugged the rails.

"How about we switch places? I'm taller, so my arms will reach farther. But I'll need you to hold the ladder. I don't like it when they shake."

"That makes two of us."

"Here." He took hold of the ladder, steadying it so she could climb down.

When her foot reached the bottom rung, her hand brushed his where it held the ladder. She pulled it away quickly but not before her fingers began tingling. The image of those strong fingers enfolding hers danced through her thoughts, uninvited. Kyle backed away and she stepped off the ladder.

"Okay. My turn." He started up the ladder and then glanced down at her. "You're slacking on the job here."

"Oh. Right."

She stepped to the bottom of the ladder and steadied the rails. What she really needed to do was to run inside the house to try her hand at kitchen plumbing—anything to put some distance between Kyle and her. She'd had it so clear in her mind that they were building a solid friendship—only that— but whenever they spent any time together, those translucent thoughts fogged. And each time she saw him, she couldn't wait for the next.

That was why she'd invited him to volunteer with her today even before they'd begun their evening of computer searches. Knowing she would see him again on Saturday had made it easier for her to leave when their work was finished. And today, she'd made sure they'd both ended up working at Mrs. Burreski's house when Hickory Ridge members had divided their volunteer efforts among a half-dozen homes.

Julia would have liked to call her efforts to stay near him altruistic, but she couldn't think it with a straight face. She enjoyed being near him and spending time with him and even thinking about spending time with him when they weren't hanging out together.

Who could blame her? Kyle was funny, intelligent and thoughtful, not to mention handsome, which she certainly wasn't mentioning. Just look at the way he'd made a personal visit to check on her after she'd failed to show at his office yesterday. Most of her friends would have left a voice mail, or maybe a text message that said, "Where R U?"

He might have taken that extra step, but she warned herself against reading something into his effort. Kyle had made it clear enough that he wasn't ready to date, from the first day she'd met him. He'd wanted nothing to do with the Christian Singles United group. He had too much on his plate rebuilding damaged relationships with family to even consider building a new one with her. And even if he were ready, she wasn't. At least not with someone like Kyle. Someone who, by his own admission, had hurt everyone in his life. He'd lied to loved ones, and she knew how it felt to be on the receiving end of lies from the people she loved.

She had many reasons to be cautious and yet she was still tempted to wonder what it might be like to spend time with Kyle, sharing more than friendship. They would laugh a lot; that was for sure. And smile. At least she knew she would. She would probably even manage to stop saying embarrassing things around him and just walk down Main Street holding hands. Her fingers tingled again at the thought of it, and she stared down at her right hand as it still gripped the ladder.

"Hey, you, down there," Kyle called from above. "I'm ready to move this thing."

Only then did she notice the piles of leaves that probably had been dropping on either side of the ladder for the last few minutes. She looked up to find him grinning down at her. She held the ladder until he was farther down and then backed away, so he could step off.

Brushing his hands together to remove some of the dirt, he turned back to her. "You'd probably get a pay cut for daydreaming on the job, but I'll keep this just between the two of us, okay?"

He winked, and her cheeks burned even more than they already were. Had he guessed what she'd been thinking?

"Let's move this down about five feet and after that, to the corner." He pointed to the first location and then the second. "The gutters on this side aren't that bad."

"That's good because we have a whole house of windows to wash this afternoon."

Though Julia had struggled earlier to lift the ladder and lean it against the house, Kyle hefted it easily, settling it farther down the roof. When it was in place, he turned back to her. "I take it you'll be washing the windows on the lower level."

Julia frowned at him, but eventually she smiled. "Somebody's got to take the harder jobs."

"You always take on the most challenging projects, don't you?"

He turned and started up the ladder again, and she again took her position bracing the bottom. Clearly, he'd intended his parting comment as a joke, but it served as the reminder she needed. She'd befriended him to help simplify his life, and here she was trying to complicate it by letting herself be attracted to him.

She couldn't risk losing their friendship. It was too precious. Dreams like the ones he'd caught her indulging would just have to be carefully tucked away. That was the only way to protect his rehabilitation…and her heart.

Kyle entered the door of the Centerville Correctional Facility, his movements stiff, his palms so damp he had to wipe them on his slacks. Ahead of him, Reverend Bob and Andrew Westin had stopped by a guard.

The three of them already had driven through the open gate of the electrified fence and submitted to a pat-down search by guards. Kyle now braced himself for the click of the door behind him. Even knowing it was coming wasn't enough to prepare him for the startling sound when it did. His stomach gripped like a fist. His heart drummed a pounding beat.

They were inside a small, square room, with

windows on one wall, two elevators on the opposite side and sliding, locking doors on either end. The two doors sandwiched them inside, squeezing from both ends.

Kyle had promised himself he would never see the inside of a place like this again, and here he was voluntarily walking inside these doors. He shouldn't have come here. What kind of person did this to himself? The room waved in and out of focus as the air—its distinctive scent familiar yet indescribable—felt too thin.

Kyle didn't recognize movement next to him, but suddenly the two ministers were on either side of him, supporting him beneath his elbows.

"You doing okay, buddy?" Andrew asked him. "I've got a paper sack you can breathe in if you need to."

Kyle shook his head, but he did drag in several long gulps of air before his breathing returned to normal.

"Are you all right, sir?"

The guard stared at him with concern. Kyle wondered if the other man would recognize him as an ex-con, but then a man tended to look different in a suit and tie rather than prison-issued clothes.

"He's okay." Andrew answered for him. "Just a little nervous. I know I am."

The guard nodded, a man who recognized that even with precautions, their safety was only as sure as the steps they took to preserve it.

Reverend Bob patted Kyle's shoulder. "Don't worry. He'll be just fine. A visit here is a bit of a new experience."

That might have been the understatement to end all understatements, but Kyle nodded his agreement with it. As unglued as it made him just to come for a meeting with the warden, he had no idea how he could ever return to this or any other prison. He couldn't handle it. He kept imagining himself on the other side of those bars, kept picturing the cell doors closing with him inside.

Reverend Bob stepped closer to the guard. "Sir, would you mind giving the three of us a moment?"

The man nodded and took a few steps back to give them some space in the cramped room. The minister faced Kyle and the youth minister and took each of their hands, bowing his head. The other two followed suit.

"Father, please bless this work in this place. Bolster our strength, calm our misgivings and teach us to love as You love. In Your Son's name, Amen."

Kyle straightened. Of course, Reverend Bob was right. He couldn't let his fears get the best of him. The three of them were here to focus on God's work and the men living inside these concrete walls. Back when he'd been on the inside, others had faced their own fears to bring God's word to him. He needed to be willing to do as much to honor that sacrifice and continue the work.

They turned back to the guard, who looked uncomfortable, but he didn't say anything about their public display of faith. "Ready?"

At their nod, the guard signaled to another man in a monitoring room on the other side of the glass, and the second sliding door crept open. Leading them past a row of offices that could easily have been cut and pasted into any regular office building, the guard stopped at the one at the end. The sign on the door read, Cal Snyder, Warden. The guard knocked, stuck his head inside and showed the three men into the office where introductions were made.

A towering, formidable man, Warden Snyder invited the men to sit and listened patiently as Reverend Bob gave an overview of the new ministry. When he was finished, the warden turned to Kyle.

"Mr. Lancaster, Reverend Woods mentioned that you served time in Lapeer."

"That's right, sir. I had to receive special permission from my probation officer to be able to visit with inmate populations."

The warden watched him with eyes that probably didn't miss much. "You were only recently released, right? Can you explain to me why you'd want to come anywhere near a place like this again?"

Kyle smiled at him, his suspicion about the state employee confirmed. "I understand why you would wonder. Until I arrived today, I wasn't sure myself. I'd forgotten how lonely it felt on the inside. How hopeless."

On a roll now, he leaned forward in his seat, resting his forearms across his thighs. "My being here, no matter how unsettling it might be for me, might show a few men here that there's hope for life on the outside. There's hope in God. That's why I'm doing this...."

He let his words trail away rather than say "Even if it is only temporarily." The warden didn't need to know that he didn't consider this a long-term gig, and Hickory Ridge's two ministers might not appreciate learning that information at such an inopportune time for the new ministry.

The warden nodded as if he'd found Kyle's answer satisfactory. "Congratulations on your rehabilitation, Mr. Lancaster."

Strange, he should have been satisfied that he'd passed the warden's test. Agreeing to work with the budding ministry had been all about proving himself, hadn't it? Yet this tiny step in that direction wasn't as fulfilling as he would have expected.

The project was about more than helping him repair his damaged relationships or even proving his worthiness for some job. This was about the inmates—men with broken hearts, broken relationships and broken lives. For those looking for God's healing, he wanted to be there to show them the way.

* * *

"'Bill went left. Jill went right. They walked in a circle all through the night.'"

Kyle stopped outside Julia's classroom and listened to a child reading fluently from a rhyming book. Obviously, whatever tricks Julia had been using with her young reader had worked.

"That's a great job, Max. Now make sure you're touching each word as you read it. Follow along with your finger, okay?"

Kyle stepped into the doorway and found Julia and the dark-headed boy in the far corner of the room. Bent together over a thin book, they didn't notice him standing there.

"'Bill went left,'" the boy began again.

Though he'd only read a few words, the finger that was supposed to track his reading progress was already on the second page.

Julia looked down at the page and then looked up again, smiling at the boy. "Now let's slow down a little and touch each word as we read it."

Helping to guide Max's index finger, she led him along the words he'd obviously memorized. "Great job. You worked really hard today. Now take this book home and read it to your parents tonight." She closed the soft-cover book inside a clear, zippered storage bag and handed it to him. "You may bring it back tomorrow."

"Thanks, Miss Sims." Stuffing the book into his

backpack, Max stood and hugged his teacher. He turned to face the door and stopped. "Hey, it's Uncle Kyle."

Kyle didn't know which surprised him more: that the boy wasn't scared at seeing him after the incident at the park or that Max had so easily referred to him as his uncle. Kids didn't hold grudges the way adults did.

Julia's startled expression could have been either from his appearance or Max's comment. "Oh, Kyle. You surprised me." Julia looked back and forth between him and Max, her eyes wide.

"Surprised? We were supposed to meet at the post office, weren't we?" After her nod, he turned to the boy who'd hoisted his backpack and was grinning up at him.

"Hi, Max." It wasn't difficult for Kyle to imagine how the boy had won his brother over when Brett had first met Tricia. "You doing some reading with your teacher?"

The smile slipped off the boy's face. "Reading's hard."

"I thought you sounded great when I was coming in here. With Miss Sims helping you out, you'll be a reading expert in no time."

Max's grin returned as quickly as it had disappeared. "Is she helping you read, too?"

Kyle shook his head, managing to keep a straight face. "No. We just have to go mail all the Homecoming celebration invitations, but I think Miss Sims forgot all about it."

"I didn't forget," Julia piped in. "I wasn't supposed to meet you there for—" she paused to calculate the figure before continuing "—twelve more minutes."

"Glad to hear that. I was developing a complex with you forgetting about meeting me all the time. I saw your car in the parking lot as I was driving by, and I figured you might need a reminder."

"Oh, ye of little faith." Julia waved an index finger at him as she gathered her purse and satchel. "Well, we'd better get over there before the post office closes. Come on, Max, I'll walk you to the front door. Your mom's probably there waiting for you."

The two adults followed Max out of the room and down the hall. The boy kept sneaking peeks back at Kyle, who pretended not to catch him. As much as Kyle wasn't looking forward to seeing his sister-in-law, he figured at least it wasn't another face-off with Brett. He wasn't ready for that yet.

At the school's main entrance, Tricia stood waiting, Anna propped on her hip. A floral sun hat covered the baby's bald head. Tricia put her arm around Max when he ran up to her.

"Look, Mom, it's Uncle Kyle."

"I see that." Tricia smiled at him. "Hey, Kyle. It's good to see you."

"Hi, Tricia. Same to you."

She reached out a hand and he grasped hers, but Kyle sensed Tricia would have hugged him if she thought he would have let her. He would have, but he didn't tell her that.

As soon as she released his hand, Tricia turned back to Julia. "Did things go well?" she asked, cryptically inquiring about the tutoring session while her son still stood there.

"Plenty of hard work there." Julia's answer was equally cryptic.

"Any changes?"

Julia shook her head slightly, and the other woman nodded to say she understood.

"Thank you so much, Miss Sims." Tricia turned back to her son. "Okay, sweetie, let's get home. Daddy's holding dinner until we get there."

With a wave, Tricia guided Max toward the door.

Max glanced back at them over his shoulder. "'Bye, Uncle Kyle."

Kyle watched until the woman and her son were out of sight. When he turned back to Julia, she was grinning.

"It's hard to resist kids, isn't it? Especially nieces and nephews. I'll have to watch Grace in a few years. She'll probably be begging me for my car, and I won't have the heart to say no."

Kyle had no problem picturing that future scenario. He'd seen Julia with her sister's child several times now, and she and Grace were best buddies. In fact, the whole Sims/McKinley family—minus Laura by her own choice—had the type of closeness other families couldn't even imagine.

She pushed open the door, and he followed her outside. They continued to where he'd parked his car next to hers in the teachers' lot.

"Max is a cute kid," he said, realizing the pause had lasted too long.

"He liked you, too."

He cocked his head to the side. "You think so?"

"If he didn't, he would have told you so."

"What do you mean?"

"Kids at this age are brutally honest, except when you're asking who used the marker on the activity table."

"He's still really struggling with reading, isn't he?"

She lifted a shoulder and let it drop. "He's working really hard."

"Was he just saying that book by memory?"

Her hand on the car door, she nodded. "That's usually how reading begins. We'll review some easier material next time. That book was beyond his level."

"But doesn't school end in few days? Will he have to repeat first grade?"

"No, but Max and I are going to have a long summer together. Brett and Tricia have hired me to tutor him. We'll make sure he's ready for second grade."

"I would say that Max is a lucky boy, but that sounds like summer school, so I'm not sure he'll think so."

Julia gave him a dirty look as she pulled her cell phone from her purse and took a look. "Well, we're going to be *out of luck* if we don't get to the post office in the next twenty minutes."

Kyle shot a glance toward his car, where the box of invitations was waiting in the back. He'd forgotten why he'd come in the first place, which wasn't such a surprise. He always lost sight of his goals when Julia was around. "Let's take one car then."

He opened the passenger door for her, closing her inside and then jogging around to the driver's side. Before, the threadbare upholstery and the electric window that didn't work would have embarrassed him, but now he knew Julia well enough to know that material things didn't matter to her.

Julia turned in her seat enough to see the box in the back. "Can you believe we're finally done with all these invitations?"

"I just can't believe we found all but a few of the people on our list," he said as he pulled the car out onto General Motors Road.

"Just twelve."

He could hear the disappointment in her voice, and his heart squeezed as he realized the sentiment was so like her. She was always looking for lost souls, or those who'd only temporarily been misplaced. Of course, it would bother her that some of her church friends had left without return addresses.

"But we found most, didn't we? And I couldn't believe all the help the membership gave us in locating everyone. They were better than a private investigator's file."

"Yeah, they were, weren't they?" She chuckled. "Hannah was an amazing resource. A preacher's kid always knows a lot of people in the church."

"Laura Sims was no slouch, either, with her supply of information," he noted. "Even if she did go over our heads, straight to Reverend Bob. Neither of us was worthy of her help, I guess."

"At least she found a way to share her information. We never would have gotten this far without her."

Kyle couldn't help grinning. Julia would always insist on seeing the best in people, even when people like Laura Sims were experts at hiding it.

"What are you smiling at? Are you thinking I'm being Pollyanna again?"

"No, you're just being you."

She turned toward the window so he couldn't see her face, but he knew she had to be smiling.

Kyle pulled the car into one of the angled parking spaces in front of the Milford post office and climbed out, pushing the seat forward and pulling out the box filled with thick envelopes. He passed by the rear of the car on the way to open her door, but she had already hopped out.

"I don't have anything to carry." She emphasized the point by holding her hands wide. "Did we really need both of us to take these things to the post office?"

"Why? Are you trying to ditch your volunteer responsibilities? You did agree that we both should go to celebrate the completion of this project, but if you're too busy…" He let his words trail away, but because he was only kidding her, he continued. "Here. You can hold the other end of the box if you want to."

"I don't think that'll be necessary."

"Well, then let's get these things in the mail."

Julia grabbed a handful of envelopes from the box and raced toward the door. "I get to put the first batch through the slot."

By the time he caught up to her inside the entry area, she was sliding the first envelopes through one of the two narrow, out-of-town mail slots.

He shook his head. "You win the first battle, but we'll see about the war."

Resting the box on the counter where they both could reach it, he started guiding invitations into the other slot as quickly as he could. Together they emptied the box in only a few minutes. Good timing because they finished just as one of the postal workers locked the outside door.

Julia brushed off her hands to signal the job's end. "That was fun, even if we didn't both have to be here. It represents an end and a beginning—the end of the project and the beginning of when we start hearing from old friends."

Kyle didn't know about the beginning part, but the ending felt pretty clear to him. He'd gotten used to meeting with Julia to go over the information church members had provided and to conduct endless computer searches that occasionally resulted in a hit. He'd liked spending time with her, listening to her stories and knowing she was really listening when he shared his own.

The time they'd spent together had been productive, and not only in terms of how many families they'd located. It had been precious, too. He for one didn't want it to end.

Chapter Ten

The organist was still playing the recessional on that second Sunday in June when Julia made her way over to the fifth row where Kyle stood chatting with Reverend Bob's special friend, Mary Nelson. Everyone adored Mary, so Julia wasn't surprised that Kyle had taken to her so easily.

"Have you tried again with Brett lately?" Mary was asking him when Julia approached.

"Not for a while."

"The walls of Jericho didn't fall the first time the Israelites marched around the city."

"Are you comparing my brother to the people of Jericho? Wasn't God against them in the war?"

Mary laughed out loud at that. "All right, smarty-pants. You know what I mean. You have to keep marching."

"Thanks, Mary." Kyle hugged the older woman as if they were old friends.

She turned her head, seeming to notice Julia's presence for the first time. "Hello, Julia. I was just telling our Kyle here—"

Julia was still ruminating on the fact that Mary had called him "our Kyle," when she realized that the woman had stopped talking. Mary stared two pews ahead to where Hannah was seated with her husband. Hannah's head was resting on the back of the pew, and Todd was crouched over her.

"Is everything all right, Todd?" Mary called out just above a speaking voice.

The young father turned back to them, his eyes wide with panic. "Hannah's...her water...I have to get her to...she needs..."

Hannah turned her head to the side so her profile showed. "What my husband is saying so eloquently is, my water broke. I'm afraid I've made a mess on the floor."

Though she'd been kidding Todd for his nervousness, she looked up to him with an affectionate smile. Her expression transformed as her jaw tightened and her eyes closed in the throes of a contraction.

Todd shook his head as if to clear it. "Sorry. This is my first time at this." He smoothed Hannah's blond tresses back from her face and then brushed both hands through his own hair. "I guess I'm failing at the job."

"You're both doing fine." Mary dropped her purse

and Bible, and hurried over to the young couple. "You just need to stay with your wife and help her to relax. Now where's your daughter?"

"Rebecca went out with Grandpa Bob to meet with members in the vestibule," Todd said, never taking his eyes off his wife.

Mary turned back to Kyle and Julia and started giving orders like someone who was accustomed to being in charge. "Julia, would you please— No, Kyle, I need you to do this. Go find Charity and get her in here as soon as possible. It's great having a labor and delivery nurse right here in the church."

"She's probably in the nursery collecting Grace," Julia supplied.

"Have Rick go ahead and take Grace home with him," Mary told Kyle.

Julia might have asked why Mary sent Kyle to find her sister rather than her, but the woman's next request answered the question. She marveled at Mary's calm handling of the situation when her own nerves were already frazzled.

"Julia, I need you to collect Rebecca from Bob and send her home with Brett and Tricia. Then bring Bob back down here to his daughter."

As if to tell them to hurry, Hannah moaned softly, burying her chin into her shoulder.

Already in the side aisle, Kyle turned back to them. "Do you need me to call an ambulance?"

"Charity will let us know in a few minutes."

Kyle jogged up the aisle with Julia close behind him. "I'll be right back," he said as they went in opposite directions in the vestibule.

Julia took a deep breath to calm herself before she spoke to Rebecca. That would be all they needed to panic a six-year-old and then send her away from her mommy.

In only a matter of minutes, both had accomplished their assignments and hurried back into the sanctuary with the others. Because most of the members had already gone home, they'd avoided attracting an unnecessary crowd. Brett and Tricia's habit of dragging behind the rest of the members each Sunday worked in Julia's favor, allowing her to send Rebecca off in the Lancaster family minivan without a hassle.

Charity raced down the aisle, part of her skirt fluttering like a cape behind her. In Kyle's and Julia's absences, Mary had already gathered a few donated blankets and towels from the storage room behind the choir loft.

"Hi, sweetie. How are you feeling?" Charity asked, already in nurse mode. She dropped a towel to the floor and stepped on it to soak up some of the amniotic fluid that left a huge, wet stain on the red carpet.

From conversations with her sister, Julia knew that Charity wanted to hear Hannah speak so she could get an idea of how intense her contractions were and how far her labor might have progressed.

"I'm doing just peachy. Want to join me for

lunch?" Hannah's joke fell flat when she stopped, squeezed her eyes shut and gripped Todd's hand so hard that he winced.

After several long seconds in which all of them seemed to hold their breath, Hannah opened her eyes and released her husband's hand. Todd flexed his fingers a few times.

"I have to ask you some questions," Charity told her when she seemed ready to hear. "When's your due date?"

"Tuesday," Todd answered for her. "Is there anything I should get for her? Ice chips? More towels?"

Charity shook her head, smiling. "When did your contractions begin?"

"Just a few minutes ago—" Todd began, but he stopped when his wife shook her head.

"About six this morning," Hannah said. "I thought it was just a mild backache."

"Back labor," Charity said with a nod. "When is the last time you ate or drank anything?"

"About eight."

Hannah glanced to the side where Reverend Bob, Mary, Julia and Kyle stood in a line of concern.

"Sorry, Dad." She paused, taking a few deep breaths before she could continue. "We'll have to have the carpet cleaned in here again."

The minister appeared relieved. "We'll worry about that after you give me my new grandchild."

"It's always about you, isn't it?" she joked, and then gripped her rounded abdomen.

"Come on, honey." Todd spoke to her in a gentle, crooning voice. "Let's try breathing together through it." He made the hee-hee sound of Lamaze breathing, and Hannah followed his example.

Charity looked over her shoulder and spoke in a low voice. "Anybody have a cell phone? Could you call 9-1-1?"

"I heard that." Hannah's voice sounded strained.

Mary pulled a phone from her purse, switched it on and dialed. When she reached the 9-1-1 operator, she handed the phone to Charity. The nurse used words like "gestation," "ruptured membranes" and "precipitous."

Kyle leaned his head close to Julia's and whispered, "Precipitous?"

"I think that means the baby's coming fast," she whispered back.

"All right, everybody, out." Charity gestured expansively with her arms. "I have to examine Hannah. Somebody needs to go out and wait for the ambulance."

"Will it be possible to move her?" Reverend Bob asked.

"I'll see if we can," Charity told him.

Todd was reluctant to leave his wife's side, but Reverend Bob guided his son-in-law through the doors, telling him he could go back to Hannah when Charity finished examining her. As soon as they were all outside the double doors that separated the sanctuary from the vestibule, turning away from the windowed walls for Hannah's privacy, a scream came from inside.

Todd had the door open again before the rest of them could react. "I wasn't here for Hannah the first time, and there's no way I'm going to desert her now," he said as he rushed through the door.

Dear Lord, please be with Hannah and Todd today. Protect them and their baby. As Julia whispered, "Amen," she glanced at the others in the vestibule. Reverend Bob and Mary had joined hands and were praying together. Kyle stood off to himself, his head bowed, as well.

Unable to resist looking any longer, Julia turned back to the window. Charity had Hannah lying on the pew and had covered her with one of the blankets. Todd ran toward the two of them, sidling down the pew behind them and then circling back to be on Hannah's opposite side. He lifted her head and settled in behind her.

Charity turned toward the glass and called for Julia. As soon as Julia focused on her sister, Charity mouthed the word, "Help."

Julia swallowed, her heart pounding out a mad pace. Her legs felt too much like gelatin for her to make it to the front of the sanctuary where Charity waited for her. How could she possibly help? She didn't have any of the medical training or experience her sister had. And what if her help didn't *help?* What if—

Memories of all her attempts to relieve her mother's agony filled her thoughts now, impotent efforts with all the momentum of a ball rolling uphill.

Charity motioned with her hand for her sister to come quickly, but Julia felt frozen. Willing it didn't seem to be enough to move her from where she stood. She didn't notice Kyle's movement until he stood close enough to whisper in her ear.

"Go on. You can do this. Your sister needs you. Hannah needs you."

He seemed so sure of what he said that a little part of her wanted to believe it, too. She nodded at him, and on rubbery legs, moved forward, reaching her destination too soon.

"Come on. Quick. Get up here."

Charity waved her forward a second time. She had put on a pair of the latex gloves she always carried in her purse in case of emergencies, and one of the gloves was tinged with blood.

"Oh, no!" Julia closed the final distance between them. "What's happening?"

"Hannah's having a baby, that's what."

Julia's breath caught. "No. The ambulance will be here in a few minutes. Everything will be fine."

"I don't think we have a few minutes. Now grab those towels behind me."

But Hannah started shaking her head. "I will not have this baby in the sanctuary. Todd, please!"

Todd turned back to Charity. "Do you think we can—"

At first the nurse shook her head, but her patient was shaking hers even harder. "If we're going to move her, we have to do it right now."

As Todd crouched over Hannah and started lifting, Charity caught Kyle's attention and gestured for him to hurry to the front. Between the two of them, they carried the tiny woman, wrapped in blankets, to the conference room where they helped her to settle atop towels spread on the conference table. Kyle hurried to get out of the way, but Todd stayed with his wife, who continued to whimper in pain.

Charity spoke in her most soothing voice. "Now, Hannah, I want you to try to breathe through the contraction. Try not to push."

"I think I have to," Hannah answered, her voice resigned.

Charity chewed her bottom lip and shot a fretful glance at Julia, gesturing with her hand for her sister to stay close. Julia nodded. They needed her, and she would help the best she could. She only prayed that the emergency workers would arrive soon.

Todd, who'd been holding his wife's head and trying to soothe her through the pain, spoke up then. "Is she going to be all right? She has to be all right."

"I'm sure she will be," Charity assured the young father. "Very soon." She paused for a few seconds, bending beneath the tent they'd built from a light blanket to cover Hannah's modesty and then popping her head out. "Our little one is crowning."

Julia's chest felt tight, and her hands could have made ice cubes feel chilly, but she stuck it out, right next to her sister. Just as the ambulance's siren could be heard in the parking lot, a new voice, and an especially loud one at that, hollered out at Hickory Ridge Community Church.

"It's a girl," Charity called out from inside the conference room.

Kyle stood outside the door with Reverend Bob and Mary, breathing a collective sigh of relief as the baby continued to complain loudly about her speedy entrance into the world.

"Sounds like she takes after her mother," Reverend Bob said with a laugh that sounded flat.

Kyle couldn't begin to know what the minister had gone through—and would continue to go through—until he knew his daughter and her child would be okay. Kyle could only imagine what a parent felt as he watched his child suffering.

Strangely, Kyle had been nearly as worried about the woman he'd sent inside to help with the delivery as he had been for the mother and child. If something bad had happened, Julia would have felt as helpless as she must have when her mother died. He'd felt helpless enough for the both of them, standing outside the door after contributing nothing more substantial than his brawn to move Hannah. Julia's influence had to be wearing off on him because this need to help, to get involved, was new to him.

The door opened and Todd stood in the doorway, all smiles. "She's beautiful," he said in an awestruck voice.

He pulled back the door enough so the others could peek inside. Julia helped Charity wrap the baby in a towel then lowered her onto Hannah's lap. The infant was still wailing, so her face was bright red besides being a little sticky-looking.

Todd returned to his wife's side, looking like a man already in love with his second daughter. Kyle had always imagined mothers loving their babies passionately from that first moment, but this was a privileged look into the heart of at least one father. Did fathers still love like that when their children broke their hearts again and again?

Hannah brushed her fingers over the damp strands of light brown hair on her daughter's head. "Welcome to our family, Rachel Ann. I'm your mommy. And this big softy, well he's your daddy."

"I'm no softy." But Todd leaned down and kissed Hannah's hair and then wiped his eyes on his sleeve.

For a fraction of a second, Kyle pictured himself as the teary-eyed man across the room with Julia as the wife in his arms, that sweet baby on her lap...theirs. *But a birth at the church?* He closed his eyes to interrupt the image. Even if Julia was crazy enough to fall in love with him and take a risk on him—and he shouldn't kid himself into believing she would—she would never wish for an unusual scene like this one.

"What a miracle."

The awe in Julia's voice made him smile. This was an amazing moment, proof that not only God was real but also that He was right there caring for all of them.

"Father, thank You for Your protective hand on our... Hannah today." Reverend Bob's voice cracked as he prayed out loud, and Mary reached over to squeeze his arm. He rested a hand atop hers. "Thank you for the blessing of my newest grand-daughter. Amen."

Glancing over at her father, Hannah shook her head. "You see. It's always about him."

She got the laughs she'd been going for, but then she turned and gave her father a tired smile. Her expression turned to a wince when whatever Charity was doing to her stomach must have hurt.

A bang from the church's outside doors caught their attention to where emergency workers were rushing a gurney inside.

"Oh. We were supposed to be waiting for the ambulance," Kyle said. He hurried into the vestibule and directed the emergency workers to the conference room.

They hurried to Charity, who greeted them by name and then said something about cutting the umbilical cord, delivering the afterbirth and giving some stitches. The three medical workers fussed over their two patients, checking vital signs and preparing them for the trip to the hospital.

Soon, Hannah was on the gurney, little Rachel wrapped in a white blanket and resting in her arms. One of the EMTs pushed the gurney into the vestibule, with Charity, Julia and Todd following closely behind. They stopped when they reached the group by the door.

Reverend Bob stepped over to Hannah, leaning down to take a proud peek at his newest granddaughter. "You really know how to give a father a second heart attack."

Hannah frowned. "That's not funny."

"It wasn't funny waiting out here, either."

"Sorry, Dad." She was serious when she said it, but then mischief appeared in her eyes. "But you know me, always going for shock value. After this, all those moms who've had babies in taxis won't have anything on me."

Mary stepped forward and dropped a kiss on Hannah's head. "Love you, sweetheart."

Hannah smiled up at her. "I know you've been busy being *grandma* for Rebecca, but do you think you've got room in your heart for another one?"

"I think I can stretch it."

The EMT started forward again, but Hannah raised a hand to delay him one more time. Kyle wasn't even sure why until Hannah turned to him.

"You know, after going through something like this, I'm afraid we can't be acquaintances anymore."

His eyebrows drew together. "What do you mean?"

"I don't share my childbirth experiences with just anybody. I guess we'll just have to be family now."

A knot of emotion leaped into Kyle's throat, and his eyes burned. He could manage a nod and nothing more. Jamming his hands into the pockets of his dress slacks, he braced himself, hoping no one else started with the sentimental comments.

"Good. That's settled," was all Hannah said.

Charity moved around them and held the door open for the EMT, who rushed forward, not giving his patient the chance to delay them again. Todd hurried after them, and Reverend Bob and Mary followed close behind.

Only Julia hung back until the door fell closed. Kyle could sense her watching him before he even turned around. She more than anyone else knew what the word "family" meant to him, how he craved it in ways he was only beginning to understand.

If she said something about it out loud, he might embarrass himself, looking like a bigger softy than Rachel's dad. Since when had he become the emotional type, anyway? Okay, he'd cried a little on the day he'd made his commitment to God, but he'd had more than the average sinner's quantity of sin to be sorry for, so that didn't count. He wouldn't have survived a month on the inside if he'd been like this a year ago.

Taking a deep breath, he turned to face Julia. She only smilcd, hcr gazc flitting to the ambulance pulling from the church lot. When it was gone, she turned back to him, her eyes bright.

"Wasn't that the most amazing thing you've been a part of in your whole life?"

"It was pretty great, wasn't it?"

"And Rachel has to be the most beautiful baby ever born."

"If you like the red, messy, angry type."

"Kyle Lancaster, I can't believe you said that."

He cocked his head to the side. "Why? It's true."

At first, she planted her hands on her hips to debate, but then she chuckled. "Okay, it's true. But I'm sure she'll be gorgeous when she's all cleaned up."

"She already is." Kyle smiled at the memory of

Todd with his new daughter, then remembered something he'd meant to ask about earlier. "Todd said something about being new at this and that he wasn't there for Hannah the first time. And I remember you saying they haven't been married long. But Todd is Rebecca's father, isn't he? They have the same eyes."

Julia smiled. "It's a long story, but yes, Rebecca's his child. He just didn't know about her until a few years ago. Hannah and Todd were kids themselves when she was born, and it took a lot of time and forgiveness for their family to come together."

"So today had even more significance than just Rachel's birth." He realized Julia had spoken of time and forgiveness for his sake, and he appreciated that she had.

"As if that crazy birth wasn't enough."

He couldn't argue with that. "She'll sure have a funny story to tell when she's older, especially about all the people helping out with the event. She had Mary running the show, Reverend Bob offering prayer support, her dad insisting on staying at her mom's side and Charity handling the emergency delivery with you as the capable assistant."

Julia lifted and lowered a shoulder as if to suggest she wasn't so sure she'd been of much help. "Let's not forget your brother and Tricia, who took care of Rebecca."

"Oh, yeah. I forgot about them."

"And you."

"Me?" He turned to face her, arching a brow. "What did I do?"

"Well, you moved Hannah so she didn't have to give birth in the sanctuary, and you were there to support me."

He started to argue, but she lifted a hand to stop him. "You believed in me when I wasn't ready to trust myself."

"It was just a few words." Yet her comment had touched him. So many times she'd shown that she believed in him. In some small way, he'd been able to return that favor. "Anyway, it's great the way everyone in this church pulls together, whether it's for doing repairs on seniors' homes or delivering a baby."

"Kind of like a family, huh?"

When he glanced at her, she was smiling. She hadn't missed the impact that Hannah's earlier comment had made on him, after all. "Yeah, a family."

"There are all kinds of families, Kyle. And this part of the church family had better see what we can do about the mess in the sanctuary and the conference room," Julia said. "You get some garbage bags from the kitchen, and I'll get the gloves and bio-hazardous waste cleaners.

"I went through training for this stuff at the school." She'd already started down the aisle, but she stopped and turned back to him. "Okay, not this situation specifically, but you know what I mean."

Kyle followed her instructions, her words staying with him as he did it. *There are all kinds of families.* She was right, and he appreciated being a part of this close-knit group of people at church, but he still longed to be reconnected to the family of his birth.

He'd seen Julia with her sister's family, and now he'd had an up-close-and-personal look at the Woods/McBride family. Now he longed for what those families shared. It was no longer enough for him to earn his family's respect and their admission that he was a decent man. He wanted a real relationship with them—one of mutual respect and shared faith.

Was it too much to ask? He hadn't even reached the point of a civil conversation with Brett. Maybe it would never be possible to share with them what these other families enjoyed. Scars could heal, but nothing could turn back time so the wounds had never existed. He realized now the reward was worth the risk. He had to try.

Chapter Eleven

Julia arrived home from school earlier than she usually did on the last Monday of the school year. That it was hot for this early in June made her long for summer as much as her students were, and they hadn't been able to sit still in class for the last two weeks.

Once she unlocked the back door, kicked off her shoes and dumped her satchel and purse on the kitchen counter, she started opening windows. The place felt like an oven, so she was tempted to flip on the air-conditioning, but it was too early in the season for that. There would be plenty of dog days this summer when she would have to sit inside with the electric chill. For now, she wanted to enjoy the smells and sounds of the coming summer while she curled up in her library with a new book.

When the doorbell rang, she sighed at the interruption. But when she pulled open the door, Kyle stood there. A large, brown paper sack, folded closed at the top, dangled from one of his hands.

"Hey there."

"Hi." Why was he here? The first thing that came to mind was that something had happened with Hannah's new baby, but were that the case, someone in the prayer chain would have phoned.

Instead of giving her a clue why he'd come, Kyle put his hand on her screen door, and after her nod of permission, opened it and stepped inside. He stopped in the entry and glanced around the tiny living room with its old hardwood floors, white-wood moldings, earthy colors and carefully chosen accents.

"This place is great," he said after a slow inspection.

Despite her curiosity, she couldn't help smiling. She was proud of her home, proud of her mother's antique pieces that she'd complemented with her own more modern choices, and she was pleased he'd noticed.

"You should have seen the place when I bought it. It was so dilapidated that I got it for a song."

"It's an incredible house. Did you do all of this woodworking yourself?"

"A lot of it but not all. It never hurts to have a brother-in-law who's a building contractor to show you how to do some of these things."

"You don't have a lot of trinkets and stuff laying around on the tables. I like that."

She started to tell him she didn't like clutter, but she stopped herself. This conversation was odd and getting odder by the minute. "Uh, Kyle, you didn't come here to discuss my house, did you?" Barely waiting for him to shake his head, she continued. "Then why are you here?"

"I checked at the school first, but—surprise, surprise—you'd gone home for the day. So I took a chance and came here. I brought Chinese."

He unfolded the top of the bag. Immediately, tangy and sweet smells filled the room, making her stomach growl. But he was using food as a distraction, and she wasn't about to be dutifully distracted, at least not yet.

"Come on, Kyle. What is it? Is something wrong?"

She studied his expression, hoping to gain clues from the anger, sadness or worry she saw there. Now the grin that spread across his face—that she hadn't expected.

"No. Believe it or not, everything's right."

"I don't know what you're saying."

"I spoke to Brett. Really spoke."

"You're kidding!" She waited for him to fill in the details, but he only shifted the bag of food in his arms. "Well? Are you going to tell me what happened?"

"I don't want this stuff to get cold."

"Then right this way." She led him through the

living room to a tiny kitchen where there was barely enough room for a medium-size refrigerator and the cabinets, let alone the dinette she'd shoved inside it. "There, put it on the table. I'll grab some plates."

When she'd finished setting the table, filling glasses with ice water and putting serving spoons in the white boxes containing rice, Hunan chicken and Mu Shu pork, she sat next to Kyle and stared at him expectantly.

Kyle surprised her by taking her hand and bowing his head. For a few seconds, Julia could only stare at their joined hands. His skin felt warm, and though he had a desk job these days, his hand was calloused from hard prison work and the weight training he'd done to pass the time. Realizing she was supposed to be praying, she bowed her head and closed her eyes.

"Father, we give thanks for this food before us. Please bless Julia and the all the lives she touches every day in her caring work. Please make me truly grateful for her and for all the other blessings in my life. Amen."

Julia swallowed hard, her eyes popping open. As flattering as it was to hear that Kyle thought she touched other people's lives, she felt honored and humbled to know that he thought of her as a blessing in *his*.

Slowly, he released her hand and reached for the Mu Shu pork. Julia rubbed her hands together in her lap. How strange that her fingers tingled as if they had a mind of their own and hadn't wanted the connection with Kyle to end. With discomfiture, she realized she felt the same way, and she wasn't sure what to do with that knowledge.

"Aren't you hungry?" Kyle spooned up some chicken, as well. "I didn't even ask. Do you like Chinese?"

"Love it." To demonstrate that fact, she grabbed the chicken and served herself, but she set it aside without taking a bite. "Come on. You're killing me here. Now you were saying you spoke to Brett…"

"I called him, actually. Last night. After."

His words were cryptic, but she didn't need him to explain how their adventure with Hannah's family on Sunday would have made him long for his own family even more.

"So," he continued, "when I spoke to him, Brett said he was glad I called. He actually said he'd been trying to work up the guts to call *me*. Big, tough Trooper Lancaster, working up the guts to call his little brother. Go figure."

"He's only a man, Kyle. No better or worse than anybody else." She made herself eat a bite before she said anything more. Clearly, Kyle had suffered in comparisons to his brother, and it would take a while for him to get past that.

"Anyway, he said that Max is having a birthday party on June twenty-third with the whole family there—Mom and Dad, Jenny and her troop. He asked me to come, too. Actually, he said Max begged him to invite Uncle Kyle."

"Tricia told me Max started asking about that right after he saw you that day at the school," she told him.

"Why didn't you—"

"Tell you? I didn't want you to be disappointed if Brett didn't give in to Max's big plan. Stubbornness seems to be a Lancaster family trait."

"Hey, are you putting down my family?"

"If the last name fits…" Folding her hands together, she sat back in her seat, grinning.

Kyle took on an air of nonchalance as he spooned more rice onto his plate. "I guess, then, that I don't feel obligated to tell you that Brett suggested I bring you to the party. You probably don't want to hang out with those stubborn Lancasters, anyway."

"Party? Did someone say party? I love parties."

She sure hoped her voice sounded normal because her insides were slamming around like bumper cars in overdrive. Okay, it wouldn't be a date. Not exactly. But he had asked her to go with him, even if it was only to a seven-year-old's birthday party and even if the suggestion had been Brett's.

"The kind where ruffians spill red fruit drinks and run around on sugar buzzes?"

"My favorite kind," she said with a smile she hoped wasn't a nervous one. She took a sip of her water, impressed by her steady hand.

"Okay, then. It's a date."

Her water took an unfortunate journey, and Julia started choking into her napkin. When she finally had control again, she said, "That's fine."

"You know what I meant, right? Not a *date* date. Just same day, same place. Same vehicle if it works out."

"Sure. I knew what you meant." Only she hadn't, and she was having a hard time covering her disappointment. He thought of her as a blessing in his life but only as his friend. She shouldn't have been disappointed by his continued offer of friendship. That's all she'd offered him from the beginning. When had it become not enough?

"Good." Kyle shifted in his seat as if the moment had made him uncomfortable, as well. He took his time wiping his mouth with a napkin before he spoke again. "I came here today because…well…I wanted to thank you. None of this progress with my brother would have been possible if not for you."

"You can't believe that."

"I do."

"Well, you shouldn't." She pushed herself back from the table, crossing her arms over her chest. "You've been responsible—you and God—for all the positive changes in your life. All I've done is to support you and pray some."

He looked at her skeptically.

"Okay, I prayed a lot."

"Thanks. I needed it. Still do."

"Don't we all."

She caught him looking at her plate where sauces covering the savory meats had begun to congeal. She'd barely touched her food.

"Not hungry?"

"Guess not."

Standing, Kyle folded the white boxes closed. "Okay if I put the rest of these in the refrigerator?"

"Don't you want to take them home with you?"

He shook his head. "I'll give you the leftovers. You haven't eaten your share, anyway."

"Well, thanks for coming by...and for the food." She rinsed the dishes and put them in the dishwasher.

"Aren't you going to show me the rest of the house?" He'd opened the refrigerator, but now he popped his head over the door. "I'm dying to see the other things you've done to the house."

Julia studied him. Why was he delaying leaving? She couldn't allow her thoughts to jump to any romantic notions again. Kyle was a lonely single adult like she was. She had to realize that, as often as he'd visited her after school or worked with her on committee work after office hours. He probably just didn't want to go home to his empty apartment and wanted to spend time with another human being.

"I'll show you the rest of the downstairs. The upstairs isn't worth seeing yet. Just a couple of plain bedrooms with original, scarred wood floors and a bathroom with that tiny, impossible-to-clean tile."

"It'll be a showplace once you're through with it."

Closing the dishwasher, she smiled. "Has anyone ever mentioned that you're good for a person's self-esteem? Careful or you'll give me a big head about my decorating skills."

She led him through the living room to the space that had sold her on her house in the first place. Through a dark-wood pocket door, she showed him into the library with its dark floor-to-ceiling bookshelves on two walls and its stained-glass window in the center of the opposite wall. Next to a worn, floral area rug in the center of the room were an equally worn leather love seat and matching recliner, plus a side table with a lamp.

"Now this I wouldn't have expected."

"No one ever does. This room was originally built as a formal dining room. You see, that door leads to the kitchen." She pointed toward the rear of the house. "But one of the early owners was a woodworker, and he must have thought his books were more important than fine dining because he built all these shelves to store his treasures."

She sighed. "A man after my own heart."

"You have to be right about that."

Kyle slowly scanned the room, glancing at her

books that weren't the pretentious library type that no one ever read but spine-broken paperbacks shelved two books deep.

"A lot of those were my parents'." She indicated the books with a tilt of her head. "The furniture in here was from their house in Indiana, too. Rick helped me refinish the bookshelves as soon as I moved in."

"Before you unpacked your dishes?"

"Practically."

"You probably spend a lot of time in here reading. I know I would." He glanced at the love seat. "Mind if I try it out?"

"Go ahead." She waited for him to sink into the love seat, and then she sat in the recliner. She got the feeling that there was something more to Kyle's visit than a thanks for the opportunity with his brother, and she sensed she was about to find out what.

He sat forward, resting his forearms on his thighs. "Well, I did come here because I wanted to thank you for your help with Brett, but…"

"Was there something else?"

"It probably isn't important. It's all water under the bridge now."

"It was important enough to be part of the reason you came." She tucked her feet beside her in the chair, hoping not to look too interested.

"I wanted to tell you about the day I was arrested." He gripped his hands in the space between his knees.

Julia nodded. This was a gift and she knew it, but she hated seeing him this uncomfortable and couldn't help but offer him an easy out. "You've already told me."

"There's more to the story." He shrugged. "But if you've heard enough about it…" He let his words trail away and waited.

She didn't hesitate. "If you're ready to share your story, if you trust me with it, I'm ready to listen."

Kyle pulled his hands apart, frustrated by his nervousness. This was Julia he was talking to, the woman who'd befriended him when she'd known only the worst about him, who'd believed in him when she had nothing on which to base that belief.

Still, he rested his hands on his thighs to keep from fidgeting. "It started with a woman."

"Probably a lot of stories start that way," she said with a sad smile.

"This one's name was Tracie Fuller. I was in love with her, or at least I had convinced myself that it was love."

Julia's eyes darted to the side, and she shifted in her seat, probably some uncomfortable reaction to his mentioning love. He expected her to say something, but she just sat there waiting to know more.

"When Tracie asked me to go to her old boyfriend's to get back some of the things he'd taken from her, I didn't even question her motive. I actually thought I was being a hero or something. A ridiculous knight in slightly tarnished armor." His lip curled with distaste over that humiliating memory.

"I never even planned what I would do when I came face to face with her ex. I was defending Tracie's honor. What I didn't understand was that she had no honor."

She tilted her head to show she was listening, compassion so obvious in her eyes that he had a tough time continuing the story. Would she still feel that way when she'd heard all of it?

"If only I hadn't felt compelled to defend her, if only I'd believed the guy when he told me the desktop computer, the laptop, the laser printer, video MP3 player and portable DVD player weren't hers. If only I'd resisted the gun when she pressed it into my hand."

"That's horrible, Kyle. It was her fault. Not yours. I sure hope she's still in prison for getting you involved—"

He was shaking his head through her whole tirade, so she finally stopped. "What are you saying?"

"I only realized how much I'd messed up as I lay face-down on the floor with my hands cuffed behind my back. Tracie was nowhere to be seen. When one of the neighbors called the cops, the *victim* helped her to escape and then told the police I was the only one who attacked him."

"He defended her? Why did he do that?"

"Who knows? She always said she could have him back if she wanted. Maybe he did want her back, but I can't imagine why. What can I say? Some of us guys aren't real Einsteins when it comes to women."

He waited for her to laugh, but she didn't. Memories of his own stupidity made it impossible for him to sit any longer. He stood and paced past the rows of books.

"I'm sorry this happened to you."

He shook his head. She didn't understand. "But it didn't *happen to me*. I made it happen with all the choices I'd made until then. It took me a lot of time and prayer before I realized that I wasn't a victim.

"Anyway, no one would buy my version of the story—not the arresting officer, my own attorney or the judge. My parents didn't believe me, either, though for once I was telling the truth. And who could blame them? I'd been guilty of every crime I was ever accused of, and plenty I'd gotten away with. I was guilty this time, too, but the facts were a little less black and white."

Kyle stopped near the stained-glass window and waited. Well, she'd heard the whole story. What would she think of him now that she knew it? She stared at him as if weighing all of the information he'd told her against everything she already knew about him.

"I believe you," was all she said, but when he

turned to face Julia, her eyes shone with emotion on his behalf.

His throat felt thick, and his eyes burned. He didn't know how to process her easy acceptance of him at his word. How could she believe in him when he'd just told her every reason why she shouldn't? Still, there was something appealing about Julia's belief in him. Freeing. To everyone else in his life, he was trying to prove he'd changed, to prove he was worthy. Julia's acceptance was free.

"Thanks," he managed to choke out, wishing he could say more. *I believe you.* Those words of support made him a stronger man, made him want to be a better man.

Their gazes connected and held. Neither moved forward, but Kyle was convinced that they'd touched. He'd never connected with another person that way, feeling content just being near her. He felt that way now, and he realized he'd always had a taste of that same contentment whenever they'd been together. There was no easy way to define it, but what was happening between them was so much more than just friendship.

Chapter Twelve

❧

On the last Saturday in June, Kyle parked on the street across from the white bungalow that Brett and Tricia shared with their four children. Julia smiled as he rounded the car and opened the door for her. As close as his brother lived to her house, she and Kyle could have walked, but for some reason he'd been reluctant. Glancing in the backseat, she could see why. Three large wrapped gifts were stacked on the seat, with another three medium-size gifts resting on the floorboard.

"You know, Kyle, there's only one boy celebrating a birthday today."

The side of his mouth lifted. "I know, but I've missed a few of his earlier birthdays. And they have three other kids, too."

"It's not necessary for you to bring gifts for the other kids."

"I was the youngest of three, remember?"

"Well, you're sure going to become their favorite uncle pretty fast."

She wanted to warn him about the perils of letting children think he wanted to buy their love, but he seemed so proud of his purchases that she couldn't rain on his parade. Kyle reached in and gathered the three big boxes, and Julia reached for the smaller three, balancing the small package she'd brought for Max on top.

They'd barely made it across the street before Max rounded the house, his church friends, Seth Westin and Rebecca McBride, in hot pursuit. He turned as soon as he saw Julia and Kyle, running straight toward them. Julia braced herself for a forceful hug. School had been out for a week and a half already, and students were often excited to see their teachers over summer vacation.

Max, though, made a sharp turn as he reached them, wrapping his arms around Kyle's waist instead. Surprised by the affectionate attack, Kyle stumbled, his stack of packages teetering, but somehow he managed to right it all. Julia might have been jealous had it not been such an exciting moment for him.

"Uncle Kyle. You came. You came," Max said when he finally released him.

"Of course I came, buddy." He balanced the packages in one arm so he could ruffle the boy's hair with his other hand. "Thanks for inviting me to your party."

"I didn't think Daddy would let you come."

Kyle shot Julia a glance that said, "That makes two of us," but he didn't repeat the thought out loud.

"Oh, hi, Miss Sims," Max said when he turned her way. "Thanks for coming to my party." The hug he gave her was gentler than the one he'd offered Kyle.

"The party's this way," Rebecca announced, her long blond ponytail trailing behind her as she ran around the side of the house to the fenced backyard.

Although Seth trailed after her through the gate, Max stayed behind with the grown-ups. He led them to the backyard. Julia couldn't help being impressed that the child had barely noticed the presents they carried and was far more interested in the guests who attended his party.

"I have a soccer cake," Max said over his shoulder. "It's really cool. It's chocolate."

"That sounds great. I love chocolate." Kyle followed him, his movements stiff.

"We have food, too," Max said.

As soon as they were through the gate, Max shot off toward the crowd of adults near a food table.

"Mommy. Daddy. Uncle Kyle came. Miss Sims, too."

Brett emerged from the crowd, a plate of food in

his hand. "I see that." He nodded at his younger brother, who nodded back.

As Brett started their way, Julia braced herself. She'd been present for two scenes like this one, and neither event ended well. But when the police officer reached Kyle, he extended his hand, and Kyle immediately gripped it.

Julia released the breath she'd been holding, and from the looks of some of those around her, she wondered if there had been enough exhaled breaths then to blow out Max's birthday candles. As soon as Brett let go of Kyle's hand, Tricia appeared from behind her husband.

"Welcome to our home, Kyle." The petite woman reached up on tiptoe and hugged her brother-in-law and then stepped back. "You, too, Julia. Thanks for coming. Now get over to the table and eat something. We have enough food to feed everyone in town."

"My wife can't do anything halfway." Brett wrapped his arm around Tricia's shoulder.

The crowd seemed to open up then, and several familiar faces emerged from inside it. Andrew and his wife Serena stood there talking to Hannah, who looked amazing for having just delivered a baby two weeks before. A few steps away, Todd paced with little Rachel Ann, who was being a fussy birthday guest.

Not all of the guests were Hickory Ridge members. Some were Kyle's relatives, and Julia recognized several families from her school. The woman with hazel eyes like Kyle's was his sister, Jenny Lancaster-Porter, who'd visited church a few times.

Julia would like to have been able to say the older gentleman in the lawn chair next to the food table looked familiar, but the man with the portable oxygen tank bore little resemblance to the Sam Lancaster from TV commercials. The smiling woman standing next to him holding Brett and Tricia's baby, Anna, had to be his wife, Colleen.

Jenny hurried over to them, wearing a worried expression as she observed the tentative peace. Julia had to respect Jenny because she was the only family member who had visited Kyle in prison.

"Hey, little brother." Jenny reached up to kiss Kyle on the cheek. "Ready for a mean game of Pin the Tail on the Aardvark?"

Though Kyle had been casting uncertain glances toward his parents, he turned to his sister. "No donkey?"

"Max has a thing for aardvarks lately."

She studied Julia for a few seconds. "It's Julia, right? Charity's sister?"

"That's right. It's nice seeing you again."

"Where are Ashleigh and Jared?" Kyle asked his sister.

"They're around." She indicated with a tilt of her head a girl in her early teens, who was talking on a cell phone. "She thinks she's too old to be here."

Jenny glanced around herself before turning back to them with a frown. "Jared and his dad probably sneaked inside to check the score of the Tigers' game."

Kyle smiled, but he was looking past Jenny, and both women turned to see what had caught his attention. Sam Lancaster shuffled toward them, making slow but steady progress as he dragged his oxygen tank cart behind him. No one cut the distance between them as it was likely a matter of pride for Sam to reach them under his own power.

"Hi, Dad."

"Hello…son." Sam stopped and dotted the perspiration on his brow with a handkerchief he pulled from his pocket. He took several long drags through the oxygen tube going into his nose before he spoke again. "I hear…you've been doing some good things…at the Hickory Ridge church."

"I'm trying." He made it sound like no big deal, but Kyle stood straighter after his father's praise.

The two men shook hands. Colleen hurried over to them, the baby propped on her hip.

"Hey, everyone." With her free arm, she hugged Kyle, managing to pull away before Anna grabbed a handful of his hair. "What am I missing?"

"Just some hellos, Mom," Kyle told her. "You don't have to intervene yet."

"Why would I intervene at all? I just want to be in the center of things like usual." As she stepped away, she glanced Julia's way. "And you are?"

Kyle stepped forward, placing his hand under Julia's elbow. "Mom and Dad, this is Julia Sims. Julia, I'd like you to meet my parents."

"Hello, Mr. and Mrs. Lancaster."

Sam shook his head. "Make that Sam and Colleen…and you'll have it right…young lady."

"Introductions are hardly necessary, though," Colleen said with a chuckle. "I've heard so many nice things about Julia that I feel as if we're already old friends."

"I could say the same," Julia said, but what she really wanted to do was to ask which things Colleen was talking about. Sure, Jenny and Charity had worked together at the hospital, but did they really discuss her life between cases?

She might have asked that question, too, if Max hadn't chosen that moment to come charging toward them with a trail of children behind him. He ran straight to Kyle.

"Uncle Kyle, it's time to play games. We want you to go first."

The boy waved a blue bandanna in Kyle's face, and Kyle sent a worried glance Julia's way, but he threw his hands wide. "Great. Let's get started. Show me where we can find this aardvark."

He allowed Max and Rebecca to lead him away. Julia couldn't help smiling when he looked back at her, feigned panic on his face. He would have been so good at working with children. A knot formed in her throat as she thought of the doors that might be closed to him because of his felony conviction. He could still be a good father to his own children, but others would never have the chance to know the man she knew.

"Max sure has taken to him."

Julia glanced back to catch Brett watching her. "He has, hasn't he?"

"Until a few weeks ago, Max had only heard stories about Kyle, and now he's adopted him."

"Kyle thinks he's great, too," she told him.

She wanted to ask Brett which stories Max had heard, but she wasn't sure she would like the answers. Though she felt sure the family wouldn't have told the children about Kyle's prison stay, at least not in any detail, there were other childhood stories they could have shared, most that wouldn't paint Kyle in a positive light. Like the one about the Lancaster children's favorite game: cops and robbers. Kyle had told her how Brett always played the cop and Jenny, the nurse. That left the robber role for Kyle. Their futures had mimicked the roles they'd played.

No, they wouldn't have shared that one, either, she decided. It would have been too cruel. Brett might have had a tough time forgiving his brother, but she'd never known him to be cruel.

"Aren't you going to join in with any of the games?" she asked Brett. Out of the corner of her eye, she caught sight of Kyle crouched on the ground as Tricia tied the bandanna over his eyes.

"Tricia and I are taking turns. She drew aardvark duty. I'm up for Bobbing for Corn on the Cob."

Her eyebrows drew together. "Corn?"

"What can I say? Our Max has an interesting take on party games."

"It could be worse, I guess. You could be having chocolate pudding diving."

"Don't say that too loud. We don't want to give him any new ideas. Besides, if he thought of that one, he would insist on diving into cottage cheese or something."

Julia smiled as a school year's worth of memories filtered through her thoughts. "He's such a great kid."

"I wanted you to know how much Tricia and I appreciate your work with Max all year and your willingness to tutor him this summer."

"You realize you're paying me to tutor him, right?"

"Sure, but I know he's going to do great because he's working with you. He'll be a fluent reader in no time."

"Kyle said almost exactly the same thing to Max not long ago."

Brett shifted from one foot to the other but didn't comment on what she'd said. "Have you eaten yet?"

She shook her head. She'd been too busy serving

as a nervous support for Kyle to eat, so now she was famished.

"Come on. Eat." He gestured toward the spread. "If we don't eat this stuff today, Tricia's going to be serving three meals a day of it for the next week."

"Mmm, potato salad and macaroni salad for breakfast. You probably can't wait."

"Oh, yeah. I'm hoping you have a big appetite."

Brett grinned then, an unrestrained expression that reached his eyes. He and Kyle looked a lot alike, particularly when they smiled.

She wondered what other similarities they shared besides the stubbornness they'd likely inherited from their father. They were both good men—kind and decent. They'd just yet to see themselves mirrored in each other's eyes.

When she reached the food table, she found she wasn't as hungry as she'd thought. Brett was acting strangely, and she wasn't sure why. They'd always been friendly at church. It bothered her to think Brett still might be uncomfortable about her friendship with his brother. Couldn't he see how blessed she was to have Kyle as a friend?

But because Brett seemed to expect it, Julia grabbed a hot dog and bun, spooned some potato salad on her plate and took a few small bites as she stood across from him. When she'd eaten enough not to look wasteful, she tossed her plate in the garbage can.

"Hey, it's my job to get the cake ready. Do you think you could give me a hand?"

"Okay," she said, reluctance in her voice. She looked to Tricia and Kyle for a chance to pass off the job, but Tricia was busy with bandannas and brown-paper tails, and the kids had a blindfolded Kyle spinning so hard that he would probably have an amusement park headache later.

Through the house's back door, Brett led her into the kitchen. A cake decorated with soccer balls was waiting for them in the center of the table, with a box of brightly colored candles next to it.

"Great cake," Julia said to break the silence that had settled between them.

Brett nodded, but he didn't look at the cake. "You've been spending a lot of time with my brother."

Julia straightened, the muscles in her shoulders feeling tight. "Yes, I have. We've done a lot of work on the Homecoming committee together. He's been a great help."

"Is that all?"

"Is that all Kyle's been working on? Of course not," she said, purposely misunderstanding what Brett was really asking. "Haven't you seen all the updates in the bulletin about the progress with the prison ministry? He's been doing an amazing job on that, too."

"I meant the two of you."

Julia blinked. She didn't know what she'd

expected when she'd agreed to help him, but she wasn't prepared for Brett's questions. "We're friends, if that's what you're asking."

"Does *he* know you're just friends?"

How could Kyle know when even she wasn't sure what she felt about him? "Why do you ask?" What she really wanted to say was, "Why is it any of your business?"

"As worried as I've been about you taking an interest in Kyle, I've been impressed by the changes I've seen in him. Everyone's noticed it. I think you're the difference. You've made such a huge impression on him."

Julia started to shake her head. He couldn't have been more wrong if he tried.

But Brett raised a hand to stop her before she could refute him.

"Please, let me finish. I'm just worried that Kyle has made these changes for you because he's in love with you."

Her mind started spinning. Kyle was in love with her? How could Brett be aware of something like that when he didn't know his brother at all? She didn't realize she'd drifted from the conversation until Brett's words yanked her back into it.

"…finds out you don't feel the same about him, he's liable to go back to his old ways, and we all know where he ended up because of those."

"Are you even listening to yourself, Brett?"

Her voice had become shrill, but she couldn't stop it. "You're talking about your brother as if he's a lost cause."

Brett stared at her in surprise, as if he'd expected her to be flattered by his words. "I didn't mean to," he began, but she cut him off.

"You need to open your eyes and see your brother for who he truly is." Never a person prone to angry outbursts, Julia had a hard time unclenching her jaw, and her nails were digging into her palms.

"I'm sorry, Julia. I didn't mean to offend you."

"Offend me? No, you're offending *him*." Again, her voice squeaked with emotion, and she gripped the counter until she could control her voice enough to speak again.

"You need to forget whatever happened before and accept him for the man he is today, the man he's been from the moment I met him. I haven't done anything to change him. God and Kyle were responsible for those changes together, and that was long before I met him."

Brett brushed his hand back through his hair, clearly frustrated with her comments. "You just don't know my brother the way I know him. The promises he always broke. The lies."

"I know the Kyle who's here today. He's a good man. He's honest. He's strong. He's like you in so many ways, and you can't even see it."

"I'm trying to see it," Brett said in a tired voice.

"God forgave him for his sins, Brett, just like He forgave *you*. Even your mom and dad are trying. When is it ever going to be enough for you?"

Having said her piece, Julia picked up the box of candles and counted out two red, two white and three blue, spacing them out across the cake. The stark look on Brett's face as he dug the long candle lighter out of the top of the spice cabinet suggested her words had made an impact. He stuffed the lighter into his back pocket.

As the taut silence stretched longer, she second-guessed the things she'd said. Kyle would be furious when he found out she'd meddled again. When would she learn to mind her own business? But for some reason, with Kyle, she just couldn't help herself. She didn't understand why Brett couldn't see Kyle as she saw him, how he failed to recognize all those amazing qualities that Kyle exhibited every day.

"Could you get that door for me?"

Julia started at the sound of Brett's voice. He'd lifted the cake and had started toward the door. Just as she pushed open the screen door, she heard heavy footfalls from the other room and then the sound of the front screen falling closed. Someone had been inside the house, probably using the restroom, while she'd been all but screeching at Brett.

The steps sounded too heavy to belong to a child, but that was all she could tell. Who'd been inside and how much he or she had overheard, she didn't know.

She followed Brett out, letting the door close behind her. Brett waited for her at the bottom of the steps.

"I'll keep what you said in mind."

Julia stared at him in surprise. After the things she'd said, she half expected him never to speak to her again. "I'm sorry I ranted."

"That's okay," he said with a smile. "But while I'm thinking about what you said, there's something you should ask yourself."

Studying him for a few seconds, she finally asked, "What's that?"

"Would someone who wasn't at least a little in love with my brother defend him the way you have?"

Chapter Thirteen

Kyle pulled his car into the parking lot at Central Park, his thoughts still spinning from an afternoon that had been both exhilarating and taxing. He could no more compartmentalize his many feelings than he could have slowed all those children who went home from the party buzzing from all that chocolate cake.

Julia chewed her bottom lip as she sat next to him.

"What's the matter?"

"Are you sure you want to return here…to the scene of the crime, so to speak?"

Kyle couldn't help chuckling over her words and her nervousness. "Scene of the crime? You know how we ex-cons love cop-show imagery."

Her wide eyes only made his smile spread. She'd forgotten, at least for a while, about his criminal record. Maybe it wouldn't always matter the way he'd feared it would. At least not with Julia.

Climbing out of the car, he crossed the front and opened her door.

"Thanks. And sorry."

"You mean, about the picnic?" he said, purposely misunderstanding why she'd really apologized. "That's ancient history."

She glanced sidelong at him, which he pretended not to notice. Her nervousness was sweet, just like everything else about her.

"I thought after the chaotic afternoon we've had, it might be nice to do something peaceful like sit on the riverbank and watch the river flow," he told her.

"Sounds wonderful." Her words came out as a sigh.

He moved to the trunk and pulled out a blanket, indicating with a bent finger for her to follow him. Past the park shelter, some older swings and a few small slides, they approached the Huron River. On the bank near the Main Street bridge, he spread the blanket on the ground. He waited for her to sit before he settled next to her.

Minutes in time and muddy water passed them as they sat side-by-side, together and alone in their thoughts. Kyle studied her profile as she watched the water. She was so lovely. He'd always thought so, but she looked even more beautiful today as he saw her with his eyes and heart.

She must have sensed his gaze on her because she first lifted her shoulder and brushed her ear against it and then she turned to face him.

"What?"

"I wanted to say thanks."

"For what?"

"For so many things, but right now for the things you said to my brother."

"Did he tell you?" She chewed her lip again.

He shook his head. "He didn't have to. I heard."

"It was you? The person in the house?"

"I didn't know if either of you heard me, but I hurried around the side of the house to beat you back in case you did."

Tilting her head to the side, she watched him for several seconds before she finally asked, "You're not mad?"

"Why would I be?"

"It's like before. I stuck my nose in your private life. I just can't learn to mind my own business."

The whole time she spoke, he was shaking his head to refute what she said. It wasn't the same. Okay, maybe it was to some small degree, but it didn't feel the same. The last time she'd involved herself in his life, he'd felt as if she'd just been acting as Miss Fix-It, repairing yet another person's life, but this time her interest felt like something different. Something more.

"It was nice of you. Thank you."

She lifted an eyebrow, frowning in her confusion. "You're welcome," she said finally. "I just couldn't let Brett continue to think— Oh, I don't know. I just thought he needed to see…" She let her words trail away, flustered. "You heard."

"Yeah, I heard."

And what he'd heard had surprised him at least as much as it had Brett. She believed in him completely. Could he say that about anyone else in his whole life? Her vehement support bolstered him. Her implicit trust strengthened him.

Intellectually, he understood that this might just be friendship—Julia's brand of no-holds-barred friendship that other people couldn't even imagine. But his heart refused to stop there. It dared him to wonder whether her words might signal that she could one day love him without any thought to his past.

"Do you ever wonder what happened to Tracie?"

Julia had asked it out of the blue, and she appeared surprised when he chuckled over the irony the timing of her question presented.

"What's so funny?"

"Never mind." Okay, she wouldn't forget about his past, but maybe she would be able to see the possibilities in his future, too. "Why are you asking about her? Are you worried I'm going to hunt her down now that I'm out?"

"The thought crossed my mind. I would have a

few things to say to her if she'd done to me what she did to you."

"You hold grudges." He grinned at her, but when she frowned back at him, he continued. "To ease your mind, I can tell you I don't know where Tracie is, and I'm not looking for her. Though I'm not looking for her, I hope she has found God somewhere along the way."

"But she got away scot-free, and you had to serve time—"

"There you go defending me again. I have my very own champion." He flexed his arms in the air in an imitation of a gladiator. "But you have to understand something. I've forgiven her. I had to if I was going to take personal responsibility for my actions. You know how the Bible says to forgive and you will be forgiven? I was counting on those words."

"You're not curious about what happened to her?"

"Okay, I've wondered, but she's part of my past just like I want to leave all those things I did in the past."

A strange expression crossed her face, and he wondered what it meant. That expression only added another layer to his confusion about the things she'd said earlier at Brett's. Could Julia possibly be jealous of Tracie? No, that couldn't be it. He was letting his wishful interpretation go too far.

Still, in the unlikely event that he was right that Julia felt threatened by Tracie, he couldn't begin to tell her how little she had to worry about. Tracie meant nothing to him now. Even what he'd felt for her years ago had only been a pale reflection to the amazing feelings he had for Julia now. This intense mingling of concern and pride scared him to death, but at the same time, he wanted to go on feeling this way forever.

"Oh, look at that."

Kyle had been staring at the water closest to the bank as his thoughts had traveled to that dangerous place of risk, but he looked up, trying to see what she'd seen. The sun had turned the western sky a soft magenta, giving the river's waves a pink cast. A gaggle of geese swam through the colored water on the far bank, oblivious to neither the beauty around them nor the role they played in creating it.

"Isn't it beautiful?" she said.

She sat transfixed by the scene before her, and Kyle was equally stilled as he watched her. Her expression was so serene, so at peace in God's world. A few strands of her long ponytail had escaped their band to flutter against her face, but she didn't seem to notice them.

He smiled as he realized that Julia was so like those geese she admired, so lovely and even prettier because she was unaware of her beauty.

"Not the only thing."

Kyle wasn't sure he'd spoken the words out loud until Julia turned back to him, looking confused. Realization must have dawned because her eyes suddenly widened. How she could have been surprised that he found her beautiful, he would never understand.

For what could have been a few seconds or thirty, they sat staring at each other, their only movement the expanding and contracting of their chests with each breath, their only sounds the whoosh of their exhalations.

His hand seemed to move on its own as he reached out to her, those loose tresses of her hair begging to be touched. Between his thumb and forefinger, he tested their softness. Silk, he decided, softer than he'd even expected. He tucked her hair behind her ear, his thumb grazing her cheek.

Julia looked bewildered, but she kept staring at him, and she didn't pull away or slap at his hand. Her pretty mouth opened slightly, as if she might say something, but it only reminded him of daydreams he'd tucked away too many times, impulses he'd controlled for his own good and hers.

Before he had time to think better of it this time, Kyle leaned in and touched his lips to hers. They were so sweet, so soft beneath his gentle touch that he couldn't help but to sink into them, like a starving man's first crumbs of food.

He touched her with lips and nothing more. Not

hands. Not even a brush of his cheek to hers. Yet his breath caught in his throat as the scent and taste of her invaded his senses, imprinting, altering everything that had come before. With a shocked moment of clarity, he pulled back, staring into eyes that looked more surprised than they had before.

"Oh, Julia. I can't believe I did that. I'm sorry." He shook his head, trying to collect thoughts that were too scattered to recover. "I read too much into—I don't know what I thought, but could you forgive me? I don't want to mess up our friendship by…"

He stopped because there wasn't anything left to say. What was done was done, and all he could do was to wait for her to say something. And from the way she looked at the ground instead of at him, he guessed whatever she would say wouldn't be something he wanted to hear.

Kyle braced himself, staring into a sky becoming more purple than blue with approaching night. He'd dealt with failure before, but he sensed that whatever she said would hurt more than any blow he'd sustained until now.

"I've been lying to myself…and to you," Julia said after what felt like a lifetime of silence. "I can't."

"Can't what?"

"I can't be your friend."

Pressing his lips together, Kyle swallowed the lump in his throat. He'd only just realized how important she'd become to him, and he'd gone and done something to lose her. They hadn't known each other that long, but he couldn't imagine his life without her in it.

"I see," he said, though they both knew he didn't.

He expected her to keep her gaze on the ground. Uncomfortable speeches were easier to deliver without eye contact. But she surprised him by staring right at him.

"I can't be *just* your friend."

For a few seconds he wasn't sure he'd heard her right. Had her addition of and emphasis on the word *just* changed the meaning of what she'd said? His pulse pounded in his ears as he heard the possibilities woven into the second time she'd said it. His mouth felt dry, and his throat tightened, making it difficult for him to speak.

"I don't," he began, but he didn't reach the word "understand." He found it unnecessary, anyway, when Julia reached over and lay her hand on top of his.

Her gesture was so sweet, so innocent, and yet Kyle was lost in the wonder of the statement it made.

"Oh, that's what you meant." Turning his wrist, he took her much smaller hand in his. Her skin was soft and her fingers laced so easily with his, as if they'd practiced this touch a hundred times before.

She'd surprised him as much with her words as

with her tentative touch. Both of her actions felt like gifts he'd done nothing to deserve. Her reaching for his hand felt like an unspoken statement of belief. Julia knew who he was, and still she'd placed her trust in him. How could she have faith in him like that? And how would he ever be worthy of it?

I can't be just your friend. Her words reverberated through his thoughts. They should have terrified him, but like everything else she'd said or done since she entered his life, they made him feel stronger. He wanted to share that and more with her, but he couldn't begin to put his gratitude into words.

"I can't, either." Those words were inadequate to tell her how he felt, but it was the best he could do for now. She had stiffened, perhaps second-guessing her impulse to touch him, but now she relaxed, letting her free hand rest on the blanket beside her. He hoped it meant that she understood what he was trying to say.

Instead of searching for any other, equally inadequate words, he pulled her close and placed his arm around her shoulders. Together they stared up at the sky, almost violet now, an early dusting of stars sprinkling throughout.

After a long stretch of silence, broken only by the squawking of geese, he pulled his head away and turned to her. The darkness having settled in, her expression was hidden in shadows where he could see only the line of her profile.

"Julia, I'd like to take you on a date tomorrow. A real date. What do you say?"

At first she didn't say anything, which had him half crazy. But just when he was convinced he'd pushed for too much too fast, she turned to face him.

"I'd like that."

She'd said yes. His throat tightened and he had to wipe his sweaty hands on his jeans. Strange, the two of them had been so many places together over the last two months—his office, her classroom, her house, church, more than a few take-out restaurants and coffee shops, even Brett and Tricia's house today—and yet their outing tomorrow would be totally new. Like a game where the rule book had been tossed out in favor of a whole new set of guidelines.

"I'm glad." He slipped his arm around her shoulders again, relaxing only when she settled into his shoulder, so they could both look up at the stars.

So much had changed today that it seemed as if it all couldn't have happened in one day. He'd been this close to women before—often closer than he'd had any business being—and yet he'd never felt this kind of nearness, this integral connection, to any of them. Those feminine faces, even Tracie's, were just indistinct shadows and fuzzy memories when compared to this woman and this moment.

Kyle realized he was on dangerous ground now, leaving his heart exposed. What if Julia changed her mind now, realized he wasn't worth the risk? It was too late to protect his heart, he realized, even if he wanted to. He'd come too far. There was no turning back now.

"You know…most people…go to the movies or something…on a first date," Julia choked out between gasps for air as she pedaled next to Kyle on what felt like the only flat stretch in Milford's hilly Kensington Metropark. They'd ridden for an hour, but this was the first time Julia had caught up with Kyle since they'd hit the trail.

"Since when are we like most people?"

Considering for a few seconds, she shrugged. He did have a point. Most people hadn't met the way they had, complete with an announcement about his prison history, or gotten to know each other as they had, with her interjecting herself into his life with what she believed was help.

"If you want to see a movie, too," he began again, "we can eat and then squeeze in a show before evening services."

"A nap in the park sounds even better."

"Aw, I was going to suggest a triathlon next weekend."

With the thought of it exhausting her, she shook her helmeted head hard, causing her handlebars to jerk to the right. She corrected her steering just in time to keep her bike from careening into a line of trees.

Kyle looked back over his shoulder. "Guess not."

He must have taken pity on her because he slowed, making it possible for her to ride next to him. "Anyway, this ride is amazing."

Now *amazing* was a strong word for a ride that had featured hills that tried to climb toward Heaven and too few valleys, in her opinion. Her quadriceps and calf muscles burned enough that she probably would never walk again, and the helmet plastered her hair to her head. Other than that, she was having the time of her life.

"Thanks for this," he said when she didn't answer. "This place is incredible."

"You're welcome." She smiled despite her determination not to. Technically, Kyle had been the one to suggest a bike ride in Kensington as their first date. Only he'd said it wistfully because he didn't have bicycles for them to ride. Julia had come through, borrowing bikes from Rick and Charity. They'd attached the bike trailer that usually carted Grace around town to transport their picnic lunch and a blanket. Her sister had even lent them their minivan because it had the bike rack on the back and a place to stow the trailer until they reached the park.

"There's nothing like the feeling when you're racing downhill, not even turning the pedals, as the wind blows in your face, stinging your eyes. It's total freedom."

She smiled. Of course, Kyle had learned to cherish the feeling of freedom other bike riders took for granted, just as he valued so many little things in life.

Julia relaxed for the first time all afternoon. She'd felt unsettled ever since last night, uncertain whether confessing that she couldn't be just friends with him had been wise. Accepting the date had been downright dangerous for her heart. Okay, his kiss had muddled her brain, but that was a weak excuse.

She worried that she was making a mistake by letting herself grow even closer to Kyle, but she couldn't lie to herself by saying she didn't want to be with him. Her heart called out to his in a way she'd never experienced and didn't really understand.

Was Kyle the reason none of the earlier matchups through Christian Singles United had ever worked for her? Had God planned for her to be with Kyle all along? She didn't know the answers to those questions, but she did know that, scary or not, she wanted to be with him today.

Kyle suddenly pulled his bike to the side of the path. Below them was a shaded, grassy area, just perfect for a picnic. Julia stopped, as well, stepping down from her pedals but not climbing off the bike.

Even though her legs felt like rubber, Julia couldn't help catching some of Kyle's enthusiasm for this place. The scenery looked as if God had painted it for this occasion, with so many amazing hills and valleys visible from this vantage point, the foliage colored in more shades of yellow and green than could ever be represented in a crayon box.

"God does some amazing work, doesn't He?" He climbed off his bike and walked over to stand next to her.

"He sure does," she answered, narrowing her gaze when she turned to him. It shouldn't have surprised her that their thoughts had taken similar paths. He always read her so easily.

"You ready to eat? I'm starving."

"In the time I've known you, I can't think of a time when you weren't."

"Hey, I resent that." He walked back over to his bike and unsnapped the screened cover from the trailer, pulling out the cooler and blanket.

Parking her bike next to his and removing her helmet, Julia took the blanket and spread it over a grassy spot that had only dappled sunshine. She didn't know what to expect from lunch since Kyle had insisted that he would take care of that part of the picnic since she'd handled the biking logistics.

Kyle kneeled with the cooler on the edge of the blanket and started pulling out plastic containers, filled with what looked like homemade food instead of the deli variety with the weight and price stamped on top. One container was filled with homemade egg salad sandwiches, another with half a dozen deviled eggs. There were even a delicious-looking mustard potato salad and a small container of brownies.

"You didn't make all of this stuff, did you?"

"You see, I still have a few surprises left in me."

She couldn't help frowning. "You can do this and you never said a word when I told you I couldn't cook."

"I didn't want you to be too impressed with me. At least not all at once." His grin was contagious. "Mom used to cook with me when she wanted to keep me out of trouble."

She wondered if he'd mastered at least part of his culinary skills while working in the kitchen in prison, but she decided not to ask. She couldn't keep bringing up his prison past or he would know that not all of her misgivings had been settled there. Those things were definitely in his past, and she needed to let him leave them there.

They served up their plates and dug in, with Julia offering enough appreciative sounds to flatter the cook. She had just sunk her teeth into a brownie that could compete with Charity's best when Kyle pulled out his new cell phone to check the time.

"Still want to catch that movie?"

"Are you kidding? You might have to roll me back to the car."

He gathered the empty containers and garbage, loading them into the cooler. His movements were jerkier than they'd been before and less efficient. When he was finished, he turned to her, crisscrossing his legs in a position that had to be uncomfortable for a muscular man.

Leaning forward, he took both of her hands, staring into her eyes for so long that her palms began to sweat, and her pulse ticked out a rhythm at her temple.

"I'd like to kiss you again, Julia, but only if it's okay with you."

On reflex, she licked her lips before she had a chance to even process what he'd said. His kiss last night had appeared to surprise him as much as it had her. Second kisses were different. They came with planning and forethought. They happened by choice.

Julia took a deep breath, and she could hear his stilted breathing, as well. Every minute she'd shared with Kyle had led to this moment of truth, and she couldn't lie about the message in her heart. Her tiny nod felt like both acquiescence and command, and with the decision, she'd never felt freer.

Kyle didn't rush. He just sat there, holding her hands and brushing his thumbs back and forth across the inside of her palms. For what felt like a hundred heartbeats, he waited, seeming to give her a chance to change her mind. And then he moved. He leaned in by slow increments until their faces were mere inches apart, his warm breath feathering across her cheek.

Julia must have covered a fraction of that remaining distance herself as her eyes fluttered closed because their lips were suddenly touching. No awkward first touch, the kiss was perfect, as if his lips had been formed for the sole purpose of touching hers. It was more destination than journey, more fulfilled promise than possibility.

She felt his fingers sliding away from hers, and wanted to reach out for his touch again, but one of his hands only came to rest on her shoulder, the other sliding up through her hair. She shifted her head slightly as he deepened the kiss, extending the touch she never wanted to end.

A tingling began at the bottoms of her feet and worked its way up to her heart. Kyle had made his place there where her lifeblood filtered in and out, and she knew from this point forward that no matter what happened between them, he would remain in that space he'd carved out for himself.

Slowly, Kyle lifted his mouth away and rested his forehead against hers. As she opened her eyes, she found him watching her, the mirth she usually saw in his eyes conspicuously absent.

"I love you."

He sat back, lifting his hands away to settle them in his lap. Surprise showed on his face, as if he hadn't planned to make that announcement out loud. His words had been barely above a whisper, but she'd heard him with her ears and with her heart. At once, she knew. She loved him. Even if she'd never suspected it before, she still would have known it at this moment as his confession captured the last, reluctant pieces of her heart.

His wasn't the kind of statement that should be left without a response, and yet the words wouldn't come. She couldn't say it yet. It was too soon. Too fresh. If feelings weren't meant to be acknowledged out loud before they'd been swallowed and fully digested, she'd only begun to chew on them.

She didn't know what to feel. She loved Kyle, and she wanted to be with him. That meant she had to trust her dreams for a future between them. But what if she was wrong about him? She didn't want to have misgivings when she was in love for the first time and everything seemed so perfect, but she couldn't deny that she did.

With so many uncertainties colliding within her, she answered him the only way she knew how. Straightening her shoulders to bolster her confidence, she leaned forward and touched her lips to his. She'd never done something so forward as to initiate a kiss—never felt the need before—but she had to make him understand. She felt his smile against her lips as he pulled her into his arms and held her close.

Julia released all her worries as she relaxed into his embrace. Later, when she was alone, she could begin dissecting her feelings and the realities they faced that should be considered without emotion. But now she only wanted to feel the peace and protection inside Kyle's arms.

Chapter Fourteen

The last remnants of daylight were backlit in the stained-glass windows as the organist played the prelude for Sunday evening services. Kyle couldn't stop smiling as other members filed in, stopping to greet Julia and him or some of the other early arrivers before taking their seats.

As he glanced down to the seat between them where his fingers were laced with Julia's, his chest squeezed. It felt so right being here with her, making a public statement about their newly redefined relationship. He liked evening services better, anyway, when they could be comfortable in jeans while they listened to God's word, but sitting here with Julia made it perfect.

He sat taller in his seat, proud that this amazing woman had chosen to be with him. Sure, he'd caught a few curious glances and even a disapproving one from Charity's mother, but most of the members smiled when they saw them together. Andrew Westin had given him a furtive thumbs-up when they'd passed him in the vestibule.

Reverend Bob had seemed a little distracted when they'd arrived, but Kyle tried not to take it personally. Instead he chalked it up to the minister putting on his game face as he prepared to give an important sermon.

"You're quiet," he said to Julia in a low voice.

"I'm supposed to be. Church is about to start."

"Oh, and I thought it might be because you were nervous about being seen with me at church. It's like making an announcement on a loudspeaker."

"I guess."

He brushed his thumb over the back of her hand to reassure her, but he didn't joke any more about it. Being here with her was a new experience for him, as well. He would struggle not to be distracted by her presence while he was listening to the sermon or praying. That was okay because he planned to become an expert at attending church with Julia in the weeks to come. And an expert at shopping at the fruit market, traipsing around downtown and going wherever else she would let him take her.

Reverend Bob and Andrew both reached their seats on opposite sides of the lectern later than they usually did, the organist finishing her last note just as they sat. Andrew sat straighter, too, and wore an unreadable expression, the jovial man Kyle had come to know curiously absent from this service.

"Good evening, everyone, and welcome to Hickory Ridge church," Reverend Bob said as he stepped to the microphone, a few sheets of white paper in his hand. Usually the minister grinned when he offered this greeting, but he pressed his lips together in a firm line.

Instinct had Kyle gripping Julia's hand tighter. Something was wrong; he just didn't know what.

"Before I make the regular evening announcements, I would like to take a moment to read a statement from the Milford Police Department." Setting the paper down on the lectern and adjusting his bifocals, the minister began to read.

"'Dear Church Members,'" Reverend Bob began. "'I would like to make you aware a series of break-ins that have occurred over the weekend at Milford and Brighton area churches. At some locations, thousands of dollars of computer equipment has been stolen, along with other pieces of electrical equipment and some cash. Most cases have also involved malicious and costly vandalism to the church facilities.'"

The minister went on to read the police chief's recommendations for church members to be diligent about locking doors and securing valuables, but Kyle could barely clear his mind enough to listen. He had the sensation of being watched, of undeserved suspicion coming his way. At least Julia didn't release his hand or he might have let his unfounded thoughts get to him.

Having finished reading, Reverend Bob slipped off his glasses and leaned in to the microphone. "I've spoken to pastors of a few of the affected churches, and their congregations are reeling from the extent of the damage and loss. Let's all remember to pray for these congregations and for the thieves and vandals who are targeting these places of worship."

The minister led a prayer for those things himself, read an announcement about the Sunday school summer party and then gestured for the music director to lead in the first hymn. Kyle didn't know why he bothered. The congregation wouldn't be paying attention to the rest of the service as members were either too concerned about their friends who attended other churches or they were craving news on the churches affected.

When church ended an hour later, Kyle had no idea what the sermon had been about, which Scriptures they'd read or what hymns they'd sung. Sometime during the service, Julia had slipped her hand away from his and rubbed her fingers. She'd seemed as distracted as he'd been.

Right after the benediction, she popped up from her seat. "I have to go talk to Charity. We have several friends at the Presbyterian church down-town, and I want to know if she's heard about any problems there."

He nodded, almost glad she hadn't asked him to come along. Though he'd looked forward to seeing the important people in their lives after they'd decided to be a couple, all he could think about right now was getting out of the building that felt like it was closing in on him. It was almost that same feeling he'd had when he'd visited the prison, though this time the bars were inside of him.

Taking the side aisle to avoid dawdlers, he'd made it all the way to Reverend Bob's greeting line in the vestibule before he felt a hand on his shoulder. He turned to find Brett looking at him strangely.

"Are you okay?"

If he looked as freaked out as he felt, Kyle had no reason to wonder why his brother had asked that question. "I just need some air. I'll be fine as soon as I get outside."

Brett studied him with what could have been concern but was probably suspicion. "Tell me it's a coincidence that all this stuff is happening in town within a few months of your arrival here."

As he neared the front of the line and his turn to shake hands with Reverend Bob, Kyle spoke to his brother over his shoulder. "If I tell you it *is* a coin-cidence, will you believe me?"

Even he could hear the frustration in his voice. Why couldn't Brett understand that he'd learned his lesson and that he never wanted to return to his earlier life?

"I'll try."

Kyle looked back at him over his shoulder, sure he hadn't heard right. Brett wasn't smiling. Those two words didn't amount to a pronouncement of faith in him or anything, but it was a start.

Once they were outside under the parking lot lights and Kyle took the breath his lungs were begging for, he turned back to his brother.

Brett looked more uncomfortable than he usually did whenever the two of them were together. "You know." He paused, clearing his throat. "I'm, uh, sorry about the things I said to Julia. I've been told you overheard the whole thing."

"How'd you hear that?"

"Julia told Charity who told Tricia—" He stopped himself and chuckled. "You know how it goes in the church information line. It's faster than a Prayer Chain. Anyway, I shouldn't have said those things, and I'm sorry."

"Thanks." Kyle felt strange, as if he were looking in on someone else's life. Now his brother had not only said he would try to believe him, but he'd also apologized. Kyle wasn't sure how to respond to both things at once.

"You sure have a big supporter in Julia, though."

"Yeah, I do."

He was glad his brother couldn't see his face in the partial darkness because he was grinning. But Brett didn't ask questions, and Kyle gave no free answers. The statement he and she had made by sitting as a couple was enough to share right now.

Figuring a change of subject was in order, he chose the subject that would be preying on his brother's mind. "So this church thing sounds pretty bad. Is it only the Milford police handling it, or are you involved?"

"We're working in connection with them, especially since some of the churches are in Brighton. I work out of the Brighton post."

"Well, I hope you find who's doing all of this."

"I hope so, too." Brett shook his head. "I just can't believe someone is targeting local churches again."

That last comment piqued Kyle's interest, but he didn't have time to ask Brett to elaborate because he waved and started toward his car. Tricia and the kids were already sitting in it with the windows rolled down, making it appear likely that Brett had come back inside to talk to him. Whether to allay his own suspicions or to apologize, Brett had made the effort, and there was something to be said for that.

Julia caught up with Kyle just outside the church entrance.

"Did you find out anything?" he asked her.

She nodded. "Thieves did hit the Presbyterian church, but the members there got off easily compared to some of the other churches. The people there just had trash thrown all over the sanctuary and lost a box of petty cash. In other places, vandals sliced pew cushions and cracked stained-glass windows in addition to stealing computers."

"That's too bad. I hope all the buildings were insured."

"We found out that sometimes it isn't enough last year when Olivia Wells was arrested for embezzling funds from our church and several others."

"Oh." Kyle nodded as realization dawned. "That's what he was talking about."

"Who?"

"Brett. He said something about criminals targeting churches *again*. Andrew had told me about the incident involving the woman Reverend Bob had been seeing, but I didn't know about the other churches."

"We're all still recovering from that," Julia said, a frown pulling her mouth tight.

She was preoccupied, he decided, when she didn't pick up on the fact that he'd had an actual conversation with his brother.

"Unfortunately, churches have always been easy targets for crime," he said. "Too many trusting people in churches. Too much forgiveness."

He'd been trying to get her to smile, but she only made an affirmative sound in her throat.

"Were most of the churches big or small?"

"Small."

He frowned into the darkness. He'd figured that. Smarter thieves would expect those buildings to have fewer employees and less sophisticated alarm systems, though many small churches splurged on up-to-date computer equipment. They would have made easy marks.

"I'll have to call my friends from the other churches to see if there's anything I can do to help," she said.

"That'd be good."

It would have been out of character for Julia not to be reaching out to the victims in this new series of crimes. He needed to follow her example and see how he could help.

"I should get going," she said.

"I'll take you home."

At his comment, Julia glanced sharply toward the remaining cars under the yellow haze of the parking lot lights, as if she'd only then realized they'd come to evening services together.

"Could you?"

"Sure."

He'd hoped to spend more time with her after church tonight, even if only to go get a milk shake. But he couldn't be selfish with her company tonight, he realized as he walked her to her door and dropped a kiss on her cheek.

Julia needed to reach out to her friends the same way she'd reached out to him when he'd first arrived, to his young nephew, Max, and even to Laura Sims, who did nothing to deserve her kindness. Her nature was to help, and she wouldn't feel settled until she'd done something.

Apparently it wasn't in *his* nature to be unselfish, though, because all he could think of was how hard the local churches' funds had been hurt by the break-ins. Depending upon how severe the losses were, they might not be able to help fund the prison ministry.

He wanted to believe he was worried about it because it would be such a loss to the inmates who needed it. In truth, though, he was more worried about his job. If he wasn't able to keep working at Hickory Ridge, he might not be able to stay in Milford. So many things had changed since he'd been released, but there were a few things he now knew for certain: he needed to be here and he needed to be with her.

Flashing lights greeted Kyle as he pulled into the Hickory Ridge parking lot on the second Thursday in July. His first thought was that Reverend Bob might have had another heart attack, and he'd even checked to see if the minister's black sedan was in its regular parking place when he remembered. A second look confirmed it: police cruisers but no paramedics.

Dread seeped deep into his gut as he cut the engine and climbed out of the car. Why here? Why where he worked with these amazing, caring people? But he understood that the why's were often the most difficult questions to answer in crime. Otherwise terms like "senseless crime" and "random acts of violence" wouldn't have become mainstream.

Looking down at his car keys still gripped in his hand, he swallowed. On that key ring hung the same key he'd been so proud of when Andrew had presented it to him several weeks before. Then it had represented trust. Now it only showed *opportunity*. With his record, motive wouldn't be hard to assume. He could already imagine the handcuffs snapping around his wrists before he entered the building.

A Milford police officer met him at the door, with Reverend Bob and Andrew right behind him.

"Kyle Lancaster," the detective began, but Reverend Bob interrupted him with a quick wave of his hand.

"Please allow me, sir. Kyle, there's been a break-in in our church offices."

Kyle nodded. "I saw the lights."

Reverend Bob cleared his throat. "Well, uh, all four of the new desktop computers have been taken—yours, mine, Andrew's and the secretary's—as well as the community printer."

"They took the whole network?"

He knew he sounded ridiculous, worrying about the computers when there'd been a break-in, and he was clearly a suspect, but he couldn't help it. The stuff was brand-new, and he'd done so much work on his desktop for the prison ministry: mission statements, Bible study material plans, cost-analysis spreadsheets.

He was trying to remember the last time he'd backed up his work on the flash drive he kept in his bottom desk drawer when the minister's words brought him back to the matter at hand.

"Now, Kyle, Officer Cole here wants to ask all of us some questions."

"Was there any vandalism here?" he asked, hoping against it. He hated to think of someone desecrating the building that so many had worked to build and where they all came to worship.

The minister shook his head. "Just the equipment." He cleared his throat again. "Kyle, he's asked to speak with you first."

I wonder why that would be. But he only nodded, resigned. He'd created this life by his own free will, and now he had to live it.

"Now this doesn't mean you're automatically a suspect," Andrew piped in, "but they have to talk to each person who has a key to the building. All the employees, the custodian and Head Deacon Littleton."

"That's fine," Kyle told them. "Where would you like to go?"

"The conference room," Officer Cole said in a clipped tone.

"Has the point and method of entry been determined yet?" Kyle couldn't help asking. He'd been around enough inmates navigating the legal system to get their convictions overturned to know some of the more important points in an investigation.

"How about I ask the questions and you answer them?" the officer said.

So much for him being just one of those questioned in this case. He was Suspect Number One because of a record he would never escape. He hated that he was tempted to lawyer up, and he was innocent.

"Sounds fine to me." He walked beside the officer into the conference room.

Officer Cole took a seat at the end of the table, motioning for Kyle to sit next to him.

"Mr. Lancaster, can you tell me where you were between nine o'clock last evening and seven this morning."

"Nine o'clock…well, we got out of prayer meeting last night at about eight forty-five, and then I drove my girlfriend…Julia Sims home. I was at her house until about—" he paused, shrugging "—ten-thirty.

"We were *talking* on her front porch swing," Kyle

was quick to add. It had been such a beautiful night. They'd probably watched the stars nearly as much as they'd talked, and there had been a little kissing, too, but he didn't figure the officer was looking for that kind of detail.

Officer Cole pushed a notebook his way. "Could you write down a name and address for Miss Sims? We'll need to talk to her."

That the side of the officer's mouth lifted only annoyed Kyle. He didn't want the officer suggesting that anything inappropriate had gone on at Julia's house. That was all he needed, accidentally damaging her reputation in addition to everything else that was going on. Wasn't it enough that they'd only been a couple for a few weeks, and she was already having to serve as his alibi?

"What time did you say you left Miss Sims' home?"

"Ten-thirty." Kyle knew this game. This was where the officer rechecked the details, seeing if he would slip up and offer a different answer.

"And where did you go at that time?"

"To my apartment. I read until about eleven and went to bed. I didn't leave there again until—" he peeked at his watch "—seven forty-five."

"Can anyone corroborate that? Anyone see you come or go?"

"Not that I know of. I keep to myself."

The officer nodded and jotted something down.

It was probably a star by Kyle's name, leaving him at the top of the list of possible suspects.

"Now the Reverend tells me you have a key to the building. Is that correct?"

Reaching into his pocket, Kyle pulled out his keys and flipped through to a gold one. He slid it off the key chain and handed it to the police officer. "I've had it since not long after I started work here. Now you haven't said whether you've determined point of entry."

"But I did say I would be asking the questions."

Kyle nodded, taking a deep, calming breath. It probably wasn't a good time to point out that he hadn't asked a question this time.

"Now in your earlier conviction, one of the charges was larceny involving computer equipment, and this case involves..." The officer didn't finish because they both knew that computers were missing here, too.

"If you've already checked my record, did you also read in the arrest report that it was about items my old girlfriend claimed were hers?"

"An accomplice was never confirmed."

Kyle nodded. There was no point in arguing the case again. Officer Cole ended the interview soon after that with the warning that Kyle should stay available for additional questioning.

It was pointless to return to his office today with his computer missing, even if the police would have let him, so he crossed the vestibule on his way out of the building. Andrew caught up with him before he made it outside.

"How'd it go?"

"He didn't arrest me yet, anyway."

"Well, that's something." Andrew smiled and patted him on the shoulder.

"The officer never told me. Where did the thieves come in?"

Andrew indicated with his head toward the sanctuary. "That door beside the organ."

Until then, Kyle hadn't noticed the yellow crime scene tape that blocked off the secondary entrance from a small courtyard facing away from the road.

"It appears someone used a crowbar to open it," Andrew explained.

Instead of heading inside the sanctuary to examine it further, they turned the opposite direction and went out the main doors toward the parking lot.

"So why exactly is the fine officer interviewing everyone with a key when the scene screams outside job, and there were so many other churches involved?"

"It must be standard procedure is all I can figure." Andrew paused for a long time before adding, "That and a couple of people who have keys also have criminal records."

"A couple?"

"Mine was a DUI, with a victim who was hospitalized but survived. It was a long time ago." He shrugged and wore a faraway look that suggested it would never be quite long enough in the past that he could forget it completely. "Besides, someone could make a crime scene look like an outside job."

"You're right." Still, Kyle wasn't going to let the youth minister get off so easily, not when he'd finally put the missing piece back in the puzzle Kyle had sensed since his arrival in Milford.

"Second chances. On the day I met you, you said you had one. Now it makes sense why you and Reverend Bob took a chance on me."

"We're all just sinners, Kyle. Sinners saved by grace." He gripped Kyle's shoulder, squeezing lightly. "We made a good choice when we took a chance on you."

Reverend Bob knocked on the glass to call Andrew inside, so Kyle continued to his car. He had dug his keys from his pocket and had unlocked the car when someone pulled up in the next parking space. Low on the list of people he would want to see, Laura Sims climbed out of her car, already frowning at him.

"I just heard about this awful business." She made a tsk-tsk sound as she surveyed the church building. "Such a shame when our church worked so hard to have these updated computers."

"You're right, Mrs. Sims. It is a shame."

"Awfully coincidental is all I can say. Awfully co-incidental."

She started away before he had the chance to answer her. What he would have said he wasn't sure. He climbed inside his car and started the engine, her words still ringing in his ears. Mrs. Sims might have been the most vocal of them, but other church members would suspect him, too. It didn't matter that the police hadn't and wouldn't find any evidence to connect him to this crime or to any at the other churches.

Andrew had come close to saying he believed him to be innocent, and Kyle appreciated even that. If he were either of the ministers, he would have suspected him, too.

Though his brother had said he would *try* to believe in him when they'd first heard about the break-ins at the other churches, he would probably forget that promise now that the crime had struck in their own backyard. Kyle couldn't blame him or his parents when they would find out and start questioning those rudimentary bridges he'd been building.

Once a bad seed, always…

No, he wouldn't go there, even if the rest of the congregation would probably rush to judgment at freeway speeds. He'd done nothing illegal, had no intention of doing anything even as serious as jay-walking for the rest of his life. He needed someone else to believe in him and knew of only one person who really did. He pulled out of the church parking lot and pointed his car toward her house, staying carefully within village speed limits.

Chapter Fifteen

Hickory Ridge's doors flew open like usual at just past noon on the day of the Homecoming celebration, but the crowd that spilled into the church parking lot was at least three times as large as the usual Sunday attendance.

The crowd surpassed Julia's expectations. Attendees headed out of the building together: older adults in their Sunday best, teenagers who'd already made a quick change into shorts and T-shirts, and young parents clinging to children who couldn't get outside fast enough. Many of the faces were familiar, but others she couldn't wait to match with names from the RSVP list.

The service itself had been standing room only, and the air-conditioning couldn't keep up with the heat from all of those bodies, but everyone had stayed in a good spirits anyway. A few of the kids had even started a nice Christian service project, fanning their parents and the strangers sitting next to them with church bulletins.

"Isn't this amazing?" Kyle said from just behind her.

Julia started the way she did a lot lately when he approached her from behind. She couldn't seem to control it let alone explain it, so she covered the best she could with a smile.

"It's great. I can't believe the turnout."

"You're surprised? You did all this."

"Me?" She shook her head. "I didn't do this. All I did was send out a few invitations, and even that I didn't do alone."

"You did a great job. Learn to take a compliment, okay?"

"Okay."

Around the corner of the building, the church courtyard had been turned into a grand party area. Three long tables were laden with the best potluck fare in Southeast Michigan, and huge floral centerpieces marked it as a place to celebrate.

"I don't know about you, but I'm starving," Kyle said.

He took her hand, lacing their fingers together, as they walked toward the end of the buffet line.

"I heard I'm supposed to try Mrs. Brewster's potato salad and Serena Westin's noodles," Kyle said. "And I still haven't gotten a taste of your sister's fried chicken."

"You're making me full already." *Full* wasn't the word, really. She felt nauseated, and it had nothing to do with any of the baskets, serving platters and casserole dishes on those tables. She felt unsettled with Kyle so near her, sensing at once the need to stay put and to take flight.

"Are you kidding?" Kyle said, surveying the spread of food. "I'm looking at this as a challenge, and I'm completely up to the challenge of trying it all."

She shook her head. "You're such a guys' guy. Everything's a competition with men."

He patted his flat stomach. "What can I say? I'm still a growing boy."

Andrew Westin passed by their portion of the line, just in time to catch the last thing he'd said. "Growing all around doesn't count, you know."

"I'll keep that in mind, old buddy."

Patting Kyle's arm, Andrew continued toward the back of the line, stopping several times to speak to others on their way to the serving tables. To watch the youth minister with him, no one would ever have guessed that Kyle remained under suspicion for the burglary at the church. Andrew treated him with his usual quirky humor.

Andrew acted as if nothing had changed regarding Kyle's job at Hickory Ridge when they all knew that it had. How could it not? How could church members not wonder whether Kyle could be responsible for all the missing equipment as well as the damage to the church door? If Andrew did wonder, he hid his curiosity well.

Unfortunately some others hadn't been as discreet with their interest, today or over the last few weeks. Since Laura Sims had made her uninvited opinions more public than necessary, Julia wondered if it were Laura's gaze she could feel on her back as she stood in line. This sense of being watched made gooseflesh appear on her arms though the day's heat was on the edge of being uncomfortable.

The serving line was divided in two at about ten feet from the front so guests could serve themselves from both sides of the table. Kyle chatted happily with several strangers in line—people who couldn't possibly know much about the local church break-ins except for the investigation update that had been printed in that week's *Milford Times*.

Part of her wished for their blissful ignorance, but even wishing it made Julia feel guilty. How could she be so disloyal to Kyle to question his innocence? She knew him well enough to know he would never have been involved in these crimes. He'd changed; she was certain of it.

Or was she? His parents probably had trusted in his innocence before, only to be proven wrong. Should they have listened to the seed of doubt inside them? And was it equally naive of her to place her trust in a man who'd only broken people's trust?

Even as she tried to tuck away those uncomfortable ideas, her misgivings remained embedded in her thoughts. By the time they reached the head of the table, Julia was sure she wouldn't be able to eat at all. Because it was expected, though, she ladled several picnic favorites on her plate in tiny servings: seven-layer salad, ambrosia salad, scalloped potatoes and Charity's chicken.

She couldn't decide whether her sister would be more offended if she didn't take any chicken because she didn't think she could eat it or if she didn't eat any chicken that she took, but she put a small piece on her plate.

"That's all you're going to eat?" Kyle asked, turning his head from her plate to the one that he'd piled high.

"I'm too keyed up to eat much."

"If you change your mind later, you might be too late for anything but the crumbs." His quip was like the ones he usually gave, but he was studying her a little too closely.

Rather than take a place at one of the long, plastic-covered tables that were nearly filled to capacity, Kyle led her to an area covered with a few dozen blankets. One of the smart ladies from the women's prayer group had thought of this: first borrowing everyone's outside blankets and spreading them out in a patchwork quilt style so picnickers could take the spots on a first-come, first-served basis.

"Are you sure you don't want to sit at one of the tables?"

"Not when I can 'recline at table' like they did in the Bible." He smiled at her, but it didn't quite reach his eyes.

Maybe their sitting alone on a blanket was a better idea, anyway. This way they would be able to avoid prying eyes and embarrassing comments.

They lowered their plates onto a green-and-white fleece blanket with a Michigan State Spartan on it and then settled on the ground. Kyle flipped his feet to the side and lay down as he said he would, his elbow on the blanket next to him and his head resting in his hand. For a long time, they ate in silence. More specifically, Kyle ate in silence, while Julia sat moving her food around on her plate...in silence.

Once in a while, she would feel his gaze on her, so she would take one of those bites she was pushing around and fork it into her mouth instead.

Kyle had cleared away about half of his food, including a man-size portion of chicken and noodles, before he set his plate aside. "Are you going to tell me what's wrong? Or are you expecting me to guess?"

Sitting up straighter, Julia took a deep breath and then let her shoulders fall forward. "It's nothing.

I'm probably just feeling the letdown now that Homecoming is here. That happens to a lot of children at Christmas. They've been counting down the days, and all of sudden it's here, and then it's over."

"No, it's more than that."

Julia looked up from the design she was creating with the marshmallows and pineapple chunks in the ambrosia salad to catch Kyle shaking his head. He squinted, and a vertical line appeared between his eyebrows. He seemed to recognize that she'd given the wrong answer, but he couldn't figure out the right one yet.

"It's nothing," she began, but he lifted a fork in the air to interrupt her. Good thing because she didn't know what else to say.

"You've been acting so strangely today." He paused and then added, "Not just today. You've been distracted a lot lately, and it's not because of the Homecoming. Your part of the committee work was finished weeks ago."

Julia set her plate aside. She wouldn't be eating any more of her food. "I've just been...I don't know...out of sorts...since all the church burglaries began."

When he nodded, Julia let herself relax. Why it was so important that he accept her lame excuse, she gave up trying to analyze. Nothing about this situation made sense.

"You're right. It has been since about that time." He glanced out across the sea of blankets and picnic tables, his Adam's apple shifting. "You know, at first I wondered if you were uncomfortable because of what I'd said to you."

Kyle didn't feel the need to repeat the words "I love you." They both remembered exactly what he'd said. He would never forget because he'd never said those words to a woman before, and now he was beginning to wonder if he'd taken too great a risk by saying them. She'd never answered, and he worried now that her silence spoke louder than her words ever could.

"No, Kyle." Julia started to shake her head, but then gripped her hands in her lap.

"I know. But it's something." No, he didn't want to do this here in front of a crowd. He didn't want to do it at all, but some things needed to be said. "Here, let's walk."

He gathered their plates and cups and stood, waiting for her to join him. After he deposited those things in the garbage, he led her around the church building to the front, looking for a place they could speak in private. He sat on the steps near the front entry and patted the place next to him for her to sit. Brushing her hands down her skirt, she settled on the step, glancing around nervously.

"It's been crazy the last few weeks," he said. "I know it's been as stressful for you as it has been for me." He reached over to her and took her hand. "But I want you to know how much I've appreciated having you in my corner. Your belief in me has meant so much."

As their fingers laced, he felt her stiffen beneath his touch, and the answers to all his questions fell gently into place. The reaction inside him was anything but gentle, though, his chest squeezing and a knot forming in his throat. "So that's it, isn't it?"

Julia pulled her hand from his, and she couldn't look him in the eye. "What do you mean?"

"You don't really believe me, do you?"

For what felt like a lifetime, she said nothing as she sat next to him, shaking her head.

"Do you really think it's possible that I would steal things from churches and vandalize church property? Particularly here, do you really think I would steal from these people who took a risk on me? You know there wasn't a shred of evidence that connected me to those crimes. And there won't be."

When she finally answered, she spoke with a small voice. "I don't know what to believe." With the back of her hand she wiped at tears that trailed down her cheeks.

Even when the jury forewoman had answered the judge's question on each count against him with "guilty," Kyle had never heard more painful words.

He'd expected questions from his family, even from the community, so why he hadn't expected them from Julia, he wasn't sure.

"I thought you were different."

But she wasn't different. She'd seemed to believe in him when no one had ever *really* believed. She'd seemed to see something in him that no one else saw, and now he found that she saw nothing worthy of her trust. Her belief in him, the one thing he needed most from the woman he loved, was the one thing she wasn't prepared to give.

"I'm sorry," she said.

He shook his head, refusing to be moved by the emotion in her voice. "At least Laura Sims comes right out and admits she thinks I'm guilty. She might be mean, but at least she's honest."

Kyle knew his words were blunt, but he'd been hurt, too, and he couldn't help striking back. He felt betrayed. Was this the kind of pain his family felt each time he'd betrayed their belief in him over the years? If it was, he finally understood why they didn't want to trust him again.

"I don't think you did it, Kyle. I know you wouldn't do something like—"

He interrupted her with a firm shake of his head. It was too little, too late. She'd already admitted what she really thought, and he couldn't let her backtrack now.

"You spend your life trying to fix people, but

then you don't trust the changes in them or even the impact you have on their lives."

"That's not fair."

He shrugged. Maybe not, but his opinion was all he had. She couldn't see it: just as God's grace changed him monumentally, knowing her had changed him, as well.

"You're just like Brett. Whatever I do will never be enough for you."

"I'm so sorry."

She was really crying now, and it was all he could do not to pull her into his arms, but it wouldn't change anything. Hating to see her hurting, he stood to resist the temptation to hold her. He'd never thought he'd feel about anyone the way he felt about her, enough to think one of those fairy-tale futures might be possible for a guy like him, but that dream was turning out to be as impossible as he'd suspected.

"I'm sorry, but I can't be with you anymore. I've worked too hard to become the kind of man people can believe in to be with someone who doesn't believe in me."

With that, he turned and strode toward his car, holding his shoulders straight. He'd thought that the hardest thing he would ever do was to walk into a cell and wait while the door locked behind him, but he'd found he was wrong. That hardest thing was walking away from the only woman he would ever love.

* * *

Julia was still sitting there staring out into the parking lot, tears splashing off her chin, when Charity rounded the building, marching straight for her. She balanced Grace on her hip, though the rambunctious toddler would much rather be running on her own two feet.

"Oh, there you are," Charity said as she neared her. "We've been looking all over for you."

Julia waved because she didn't trust herself to speak. Her sister must not have noticed that she'd been crying because she chatted on happily.

"Did you bring anything to change into for co-ed softball? I hope Kyle's a good player because we both know you're not. Or we could play horseshoes. Wait." Charity stopped and surveyed the scene for the first time before turning back to Julia. "First, why are you crying, and second, where's Kyle?"

"He's gone." She managed to answer both questions with two words and the gasp that escaped her mouth along with them.

Charity sat beside Julia, sandwiching Grace between them as she pulled her into her arms. Grace let out a whine of protest that the two of them would have laughed at under usual circumstances.

"What happened, sweetie?" Charity pulled away slightly and drew her daughter onto her lap.

"I love him." Again Julia's voice cracked as she spoke.

The side of Charity's mouth lifted, but her eyes remained sad. "Of course you do." Her gaze narrowed. "That's why he left?"

Julia shook her head, too guilt-ridden and confused to be able to explain what had happened. "I couldn't...believe in him."

She didn't say more, and yet Charity nodded, seeming to understand. "Do you want to talk about it?"

"I can't. Not yet."

"Okay. I'm available whenever you're ready."

On Charity's lap, Grace squirmed so her mother let her down in the garden area near the steps. Immediately, Grace took off toward the parking lot, her mother at her heels. Once she had the child's hand, Charity turned back to Julia.

"Do you want to come back to the celebration?"

Julia shook her head. "I think I'm going to go home."

"That's too bad. You've worked so hard on the celebration."

"It's turning out differently than I expected," Julia said with a shrug.

"You can say that again. Here you are in tears, and I just passed Mother, and she was crying, too. Reverend Bob took her inside to counsel her."

Kyle had mentioned Laura Sims, too. He'd called her "honest" for at least admitting she thought he was guilty. Julia hadn't even been honest with herself for the longest time. Now that she could admit she wanted a life with Kyle, she'd done everything she could to lose that possibility.

"Hey, I've got to get back. Are you going to be okay?" Charity asked, waiting for her nod before she lifted Grace and started back toward the church courtyard. Over her shoulder, she said, "I'm sure everything's going to turn out all right...for my mother and for you and Kyle."

As Julia started for her car, she decided that her sister, who was seldom wrong, had to be mistaken this time. Whatever chance she'd had for a future with Kyle she'd destroyed by her own inability to believe in him. He deserved someone better than her, anyway. Someone who trusted without conditions. Someone who didn't hold the people she loved under the weight of her expectations.

Julia climbed into her car and started toward her house. She couldn't call it a home right now and maybe wouldn't ever again. In the rearview mirror, she caught sight of the Homecoming festivities. She'd planned for this day for months. The idea of past members *coming home* to a place where their faith was nurtured was so appealing. She didn't miss the irony in the scene behind her: she was leaving a place of "homecoming" and she'd never felt more lost.

Chapter Sixteen

Kyle paced back and forth in his apartment late the next afternoon, becoming more agitated by the few strides it took him to cross from one side to the other. He'd been crawling out of his skin ever since leaving Julia and the celebration that had been anything but festive for him. His apartment only made the situation worse, its walls closing in around him, its silence mocking him.

He'd been naive to believe a future might be possible between him and Julia. And maybe it had been too much for him to ask for total belief from *anyone* who knew about his past. He pressed his hand against his chest, his heart squeezing. The thought of a life without Julia loomed before him like a road that spread endlessly in two directions, neither more appealing than the other.

He paced back again and stopped by the window

that overlooked the tree-lined street. Instead of calming him, looking out only made him feel more contained. He'd spent all last evening in his apartment, and he'd been home from work less than an hour today, and already he knew he couldn't stay here a minute longer.

He might not be able to do anything to change what had happened with Julia, but he knew of something he could do that would be more productive than hanging around feeling sorry for himself. It not only would fill up some of the empty nights he predicted in his near future, but it might help some local people at the same time.

Before he could change his mind and settle back for another session of pity-partying, he grabbed his car keys and headed out the door. He took the most direct route up Main Street and arrived at his destination only minutes later. He didn't waste time worrying how his offer would be received. It was the right thing to do, and sometimes that right thing came at a cost.

At the front door of the familiar white bungalow, he knocked loudly. He heard youthful voices and chaos from inside the house, but it was Brett who opened the door. Already off the day shift at the state police post, he was dressed in jeans and a Beatles T-shirt.

"Kyle?" His eyebrow lifted, but he automatically opened the screen and backed away to allow him to enter.

"Who is it, Brett?" Tricia called from the living room.

"Kyle," he said unnecessarily, since she was already standing there looking at him.

"Oh, hi, Kyle. We were just sitting down to dinner. Would you like to stay?" She turned her head toward the kitchen where Anna could be seen in her high chair banging on the tray with a spoon. From the noise coming from the kitchen, the other three were probably already seated at the table behind the wall.

"Yeah, um…want to have dinner with us?" Brett repeated the offer.

"No. Thanks, though." By now, they'd probably heard about his breakup with Julia, and though he appreciated the offer, he wasn't ready to deal with the questions. He wasn't ready to talk about her yet. "I just wanted to speak to Brett for a few minutes. I can come back later," he added in a rush.

"Is that Uncle Kyle?" Max came running from the kitchen, a fork in his hand. "Hi, Uncle Kyle."

"Hey, Max."

Brett turned to the boy. "All right. Head back into the kitchen with your mom, Max. I'm going to talk to my brother for a few minutes."

Max frowned, planting his hands on his hips. "What about prayers?"

"You can lead this time."

That seemed to satisfy him, so he followed Tricia to the rear of the house.

"Here, let's talk on the porch." Brett led Kyle outside where he sat on the step and waited.

Rather than sit, Kyle descended the three steps and stood to face him from the landing. "I wanted to talk to you about the church break-ins."

Brett took a deep breath and held it, his shoulders and his jaw tight, as if he were preparing for the worst.

"No, this isn't a confession."

The police officer's shoulders came forward with what could only have been a sigh of relief. "Sorry about that. It was just habit."

"Don't worry about it. I know it's going to take time, but one of these days you won't jump to those kinds of conclusions about me anymore."

"I hope you're right." Brett stretched his hand across his face, pressing his temples with his thumb and longest finger. "Now, you were saying…"

"Let me help you catch the guys."

Brett was already shaking his head, but he still said, "What are you saying?"

"Let's just say that I have a certain amount of *expertise* from my juvenile delinquent days that might help you." Before his brother could ask, he added, "No, I never broke into any churches. But I can't say the same thing about other buildings."

Again Brett shook his head. "I doubt your *expertise* could help."

"Why don't you hear me out and see?" Kyle

crossed his arms over his chest. "What if I were to tell you that although the vandalism appears to be the work of juveniles, these break-ins probably aren't juvenile crimes?"

"Why would you say that?"

"Because in juvenile crime, the thrill is a good part of the attraction. And what thrill could there be in repeating the same crime over and over? The vandalism isn't even getting more creative each time. Just the same dull destruction."

"Okay, I'll bite. But why can't the thrill be in just not getting caught?"

"Because the stakes would need to be getting higher to keep the thrill going. By now I would expect them to be painting messages on the church walls like, 'Catch me if you can' rather than just continue to slash pew cushions and damage sound systems."

"You might be right."

Kyle stared at his brother, sure he hadn't heard him right. "Me? Right?"

"Don't push it, okay, but you might have something there. The investigation's been off-course for a while."

Though he didn't say it, Kyle knew he meant since the break-in at their church when Kyle had become a suspect. "The suspects just got lucky when they hit Hickory Ridge where a recent parolee happened to work. I was too easy a target for suspicion."

Brett glanced at the front door behind him, then he

turned back to Kyle. "I have to get in there before those kids eat all the pork chops, but why don't we do this... I'm meeting my former partner, Trooper Joe Rossetti, for coffee at Klancy's at seven. He's working the two-to-ten shift. Why don't you meet us there?"

Kyle's eyes widened. Brett had surprised him by accepting his offer of help.

Brett nodded as if to confirm that he really meant it. "We've had more break-ins in Milford and in Livingston County. Maybe the M.P.D. and the Brighton post troopers need to look in a new direction."

"Good. I'll meet you there."

With a wave, Kyle started down the walk toward his car.

"Kyle?"

He turned back to see Brett still standing on the porch. "I heard about you and Julia. I'm sorry."

"Thanks." He fought back the lump that appeared in his throat at even the thought of her.

"If she doesn't come back, it will be her loss. You're a good man. She told me that herself." He paused, looking at the ground before meeting Kyle's gaze again. "It just took me a lot longer to see it."

For a long time after his brother went inside to finish dinner with his family, Kyle sat in his car replaying their conversation. Something had shifted in his life, and he felt God's blessing in His timing. Maybe his life would not turn out the way he'd hoped since meeting Julia, but that didn't mean he wouldn't be able to build a life of some kind. Surrounded by people who'd never stopped loving him even when he'd disappointed them, he would have the support he needed to survive.

"Goodbye, Miss Sims," Max yelled out the minivan window as Tricia pulled away from the curb in front of Julia's house. "Thanks for the reading."

Through the van's tinted side windows, Julia couldn't even see his face, but she could see some tiny fingers sticking out through the edge of the pop-open window. She waved. It had been a great tutoring session, one of those teachable moments where things clicked for Max, who'd made some necessary connections that would help him become a strong reader.

At first, Julia had been worried when Tricia had phoned to set up this week's tutoring session—Max was one of Kyle's biggest fans, after all—but it had given her a welcome escape from living in the summer break prison of her own thoughts. Even enduring Tricia's sympathetic looks and Max's questions hadn't been as tough as she predicted or as painful as her own introspection had been the past five days.

Once the van was out of sight, she crossed to the

porch swing that had been one of her reasons for choosing the house and settled on it, turning herself sideways so she could rest her feet on the other end. The swing reminded her of Kyle now, but that shouldn't have surprised her since everything did lately.

Her chest squeezed with longing as it did every time she thought of him. And with every thought, her heart shattered into even more pieces. She'd lost Kyle, and she had no one to blame but herself. He hadn't asked for much from her, only a little belief and some simple trust, the things he needed most and the things she was least equipped to give.

Closing her eyes, she shifted her head and shoulders so the swing would begin to sway. Its rhythm soothed her, while the breeze it created cut a little into the steamy August heat. With her eyes closed, she only pictured Kyle's face again, so she gave up and opened them again.

It was ironic that she'd first approached Kyle because she'd thought she could help *him* get his life together. That was like the patient on the heart transplant list trying to heal the other patient awaiting a tonsillectomy. It felt like the height of arrogance now that she realized God had probably sent Kyle into her life to help her.

From the beginning, Kyle had been right about her. He'd known immediately something it had taken nearly twenty years to realize: she tried to fix people because *she* was broken. It seemed so clear now. Why had it been so hard for her to see?

She'd always thought of helping people as her calling, but she understood now it was also her crutch. She used reaching out to others as a way of controlling her world, a way to prevent feeling as out of control as she'd felt during her mother's illness and after discovering her father's secret second family. But though Julia reached out, she held people at a careful distance, unable to trust them not to fail her or to leave her as her mother had, whether she'd intended to or not.

Now that Julia had discovered the truth about herself, she wasn't sure what to do with the information. Did it mean that, in order to release control, she should stop helping?

"You really are a mess, aren't you?" Julia said to the empty space around her as she wiped the tears that had come in regular intervals during her path to discovery. She was so tired of crying, so tired of feeling like this.

"Not any more than the rest of us, I suppose."

Julia startled at the sound of a woman's voice and turned her head toward it. She blinked at the sight before her, convinced her eyes were playing tricks on her. But when she opened her eyes again, Laura Sims still stood there, looking nervous.

"Mrs. Sims?" Even speaking Laura's name seemed strange to Julia. The same woman who shared a last name with her but hadn't had a civil thing to say to her in the six years they'd known each other stood on her porch.

Julia drew her legs down from the swing and stood to face her uninvited guest. "Is there something I can help you with?"

"You probably weren't expecting to see me."

"Well, it is a surprise." She shot a glance to the road but didn't see Laura's easily recognizable silver Cadillac parked out there.

"It shouldn't be a surprise for one church member to visit another."

"No...it shouldn't." Julia took a deep breath and dropped back onto the swing, preparing herself for another of Laura Sims's lectures. Usually she weathered them as well as any other Hickory Ridge member, but today wasn't like other days. "You know, Mrs. Sims, this might not be the best time for a visit, after all."

Instead of backing down the steps, Laura crossed the porch and stood in front of Julia. Her bearing wasn't as commanding as usual, and she seemed to stare at the toes of her shoes. "The way I've always heard it, there's never a bad time to say you're sorry."

Julia was already shaking her head, predicting that Laura would argue, but she wasn't prepared for a comment like that. "Excuse me?"

"I've come to apologize. I'm sorry for the way

I've treated you since you came to Milford to be near your sis—to be with Charity."

"I don't understand."

Laura smiled, her eyes bright with unshed tears. "I wouldn't expect you to. I've been so horrible to everyone. You most of all."

She gestured toward the swing, and at Julia's nod, she lowered herself onto it. Several seconds passed as she stared out at the street.

"I thought I knew God," she began. "I always talked about His judgments. It was easy to see that side of Him when I was so angry with my life. But I didn't know the loving and forgiving God who Reverend Bob told us about."

She paused, a huge smile appearing on her face. "On Sunday, I met Him for the first time."

"That's wonderful, Mrs. Sims." Julia managed to keep her surprise from showing in her expression.

"Don't you think after all these years you could call me Laura?" At Julia's wide-eyed expression, Laura chuckled. "Okay, we'll work on that. Anyway, I wanted to apologize, and I wanted to thank you for being kind to me when I didn't deserve it. You were always a reflection of God's love, even to someone as unlovable as I was."

The tears came so quickly that Julia didn't have time to control them. Strange, she hadn't thought she'd had any tears left to cry, and yet here they were.

Unpracticed at providing comfort, Laura leaned

over and patted her shoulder awkwardly. "What is it...dear?"

"My love isn't anything like God's love. Mine comes with strings."

"This is about Kyle Lancaster, isn't it? I heard about your breakup."

Julia looked up though she shouldn't have been surprised that their breakup had become common knowledge. The birth of their relationship had happened in front of the Hickory Ridge community, so it wasn't unexpected that the end would be equally public.

"If I've learned anything about love, and admittedly it's taken me a while to learn it, real love comes with forgiveness," Laura said.

"How could Kyle ever forgive me? I couldn't believe in him when that was the one thing he needed from me. How can he have faith in me again, knowing that even I questioned his innocence?"

"He also knows you love him." At Julia's sharp glance, she smiled. "It wasn't a secret to anyone who saw the two of you together. Your feelings or his."

Julia shrugged, the pain inside feeling fresh again. She knew Kyle loved her. He'd told her so, and she would never forget the joy in hearing him speak those words. He'd said he couldn't be with someone who didn't believe in him, and she prayed she would one day learn to trust him without holding back a shred of doubt, but she couldn't offer a guarantee. They were at an impasse.

"It's probably too late."

"Forgiveness sometimes takes time. Ask your sister about that one. Just give Kyle some time. If he loves you, he'll find a way to forgive you."

Laura smiled as she rested her head on the back of the swing. She'd been privileged to receive Charity's forgiveness. Healing, though, had been a much slower process.

Still, Julia liked the reminder she found in Laura's story. If Charity could forgive her mother, though Laura's lies had denied her precious years with her father and even prevented her from knowing her sister until they were both adults, then maybe there was hope for others who'd made mistakes. Maybe one day, Kyle could forgive her, too.

Chapter Seventeen

Kyle was sitting at his desk doing research on a newly donated computer when he heard a racket behind him. He turned to find his quiet private office neither quiet nor private. Brett stood there in full State Police uniform, but he was flanked by their mother and sister on one side and Tricia on the other.

"What's wrong?" Thoughts of his father's weakened state had him coming out of his chair and rushing around his desk to the others.

"You mean, who's right, don't you, son?" Sam Lancaster sat in his new battery-powered wheelchair, having taken the recently installed elevator to get to the second floor.

"What are you talking about, and why are you all here?" Kyle crossed his arms over his chest. "Please tell me this isn't a family intervention or something."

"Only the best kind." Colleen grinned over at her son.

Kyle frowned. "Somebody needs to fill me in on the joke here."

Instead of answering, everyone turned to Brett, who stepped forward. "I wanted to let you know that there's been an arrest in the church break-ins. A couple of guys from South Lyon are cooling their hills in Oakland County Jail. A couple of *middle-aged guys* who had a house full of electronics."

"That's great that you made an arrest. Thanks for telling me, but why the entourage?" He gestured with his hand toward his office phone. "You could have called, you know."

"Why would I do something as simple as that?" At Kyle's frown, Brett continued. "I just wanted to tell you in person that your suggestions for the investigation led directly to the arrest. I'm here to say thank-you."

"Did you bring everyone to be the audience while you present my cash reward?" At first, Kyle didn't know whether to be flattered or offended by the fuss but decided to take it as Brett probably hoped he would: as a show of support.

"Sorry. No cash reward. Only the undying gratitude of the Milford Police Department and the Michigan State Police."

"What would I do with cash anyway? You know, food, rent and utilities—they're so overrated."

Everyone laughed at that, and everything seemed right in the Lancaster family for the first time in a long time. He couldn't help wondering what Julia would have thought of this scene, almost as cheesy as her picnic scam. She'd been a part of helping him restore his family relationships, and it seemed wrong for her to miss this.

But it wasn't just this moment where he'd felt her absence. So many times she'd come to mind this week—when additional funding came through for the prison ministry, when the article about the "Homecoming" appeared in the *Milford Times*, even when Max ran up to him at church to tell him how well he was reading. So often he'd lifted the phone to call her and had driven by her house, his foot tempted to brake.

All those around him were laughing again when Sam rolled his chair over to Kyle. "Son, pay attention. I wanted to tell you how proud we are of you. Not just for this but for everything since you've, ah, come to Milford."

"Thanks, Dad." Kyle couldn't help smiling, knowing it would always be difficult for his father to discuss Kyle's incarceration. What he'd said mattered more, anyway. It had been a long journey back, but the prodigal son had finally been welcomed home.

"And tomorrow I would like you to come down to my office where we can talk about your future with the dealership."

"Are you serious?" He'd waited so long to hear this, had imagined so many times how it would sound like when his father finally recognized his worth and made the offer.

"Probably too serious," his sister Jenny chimed in. "In six months, Kyle, when you're hating all this, remember it was your idea."

"Why do you think I carry a badge?" Brett said with a laugh. "The alternative of working for Dad again was too scary to imagine."

"Thanks a lot, you two." Then to his father he said, "Thanks, Dad. I look forward to discussing this with you."

As he showed his family out of his office and returned to his desk, he found it strange that he wasn't anticipating that meeting with his father more than he was. He'd worked so hard and planned so long for this single goal, and yet now that he was close to achieving it, the victory felt like an empty one.

But he hadn't accounted for Julia Sims in those plans. Nothing could have prepared him for her entrance into his life, the shift in his world that she would create. Without her now, that world seemed to be riddled with holes.

But she hadn't believed in him completely, he reminded himself. She hadn't accused him of being guilty of the church invasions, but she hadn't been certain of his innocence, either.

Can you blame her? The question echoed in his ears. The ink had been barely dry on his prison release papers when he'd met her, and the first things she'd learned about him were his many failures, and yet she'd found a way to trust him. Why had he held her to an impossible standard of belief when he'd done nothing to earn it? And how could he expect perfection from her when by choosing him, she'd found a flawed man at best?

With a glance at the digital clock on the lower right corner of his computer monitor, he powered down the machine and closed up his office. He had a lot of thinking to do before he spoke with his father again tomorrow. The business—the thing he thought he wanted most—was within his reach, but he wondered now if it would be enough if he didn't have the person or the life he truly needed.

The morning fog had yet to burn off over Milford Township when Julia climbed the outside stairs to Kyle's downtown apartment. It was too early in the morning for anyone to receive guests, even welcome ones, but she couldn't wait any longer. She knocked before she could talk herself out of it.

Kyle pulled open the door, his hair wet from a recent shower and his shirt misbuttoned over his white undershirt as if he'd dressed in a rush. Of course, he would be getting ready for work. That was what most normal people did at this hour of the morning.

His eyes went wide. "Julia, are you all right?"

Until he asked, she hadn't realized that she'd gone out of her house in the same clothes she'd worn the day before. Realizing she hadn't even bothered to comb her hair, she patted it but finally gave up. "I'm sorry. I must look terrible."

"You look fine, but you didn't answer my question." His hands reached out to her, but he stopped just before they landed on her shoulders.

"I'm okay. But I'd really like to talk to you."

"All right." Not giving away anything with his blank expression, he backed inside his apartment and gestured for her to come inside. "It's not quite as spacious as your place."

She took in the tight space and sparse furnishings, taking note of the family portrait and a few outdoor prints on the walls. "I like this place. It's nice."

"Want breakfast? I was about to make some eggs." As he spoke, he rebuttoned his shirt.

"Maybe just coffee?" She couldn't imagine trying to get eggs down as unsteady as her stomach was, but she didn't tell him that.

"Good idea," he said, and then yawned. "I was talking on the phone pretty late last night." He led her into a tiny galley kitchen where a coffeemaker was already brewing. He waved her toward one of the two seats at the card table. Instead of moving to the stove, he filled two mugs, carried them to the table and sat across from her.

Julia didn't know where to begin. She'd had so many things to say to him, and now that she could, none of them came easily. She gripped her hands together, resting her forearms on the table.

"You said you wanted to talk," Kyle said finally.

She could have apologized again. She could have started slowly and built to the most important things she wanted to say, but Julia decided to start at the top. "I'm ready now."

Kyle had lifted his coffee mug to his lips, but he lowered it without taking a sip. "Ready?"

"I wasn't ready to trust you before, but I am now. I believe in you, and I won't let you down again."

He opened his mouth as if to argue, but she raised her hand to stop him. No matter what he said later, she needed him to know what she was feeling.

"I love you, Kyle." Though she'd been so afraid to say those words, she felt empowered by them now. She found strength in facing her weakness. "I've known that for a long time, though it terrified me to realize it. I want to be there for you. You can know you have my complete trust, even if your family never accepts you again."

She didn't know how she expected Kyle to react, but she wasn't prepared for him to start shaking his head that way, as if it were too late. As if hope were gone.

"You can't know that you'll never let someone down. Nobody can make a promise like that," he told her.

A lump appearing in her throat and her eyes dampening, Julia heard the pleading tone in her voice as she tried again. "But I know you're innocent. Deep in my heart, I always knew. I don't know what made me question it."

Kyle shook his head again. "It was too much to ask. I should never have expected it of you."

Julia stopped, her eyebrows drawing together. "What are you saying?"

"It wasn't fair of me. I should have known how hard it would be for you to really trust, even the people you love. Your dad lied to you, and your mom died and left you." He shrugged. "Trust isn't something that can be demanded, anyway. You have to earn it. You'd already given me a gift by having faith in me when so many didn't, and I had to ask for more than you could give."

"But I can give it. I know I can." She sounded desperate, but she couldn't seem to stop herself. "And you don't need your dad's dealership, either. We'd be okay. Please. You know as long as we're together, we'll be just fine."

Finally, Kyle reached across the table and lay his hand across hers, causing her to stop wringing them. "Julia, you're not listening to me."

Her eyes burned. She could survive this, she

reminded herself. She'd done all she could by taking a risk and putting her heart on the line. Now if Kyle rejected her, she would simply have to trust that God would someday ease the pain.

"Go ahead," she said, feeling resigned.

"First, I hope you're serious about not caring if I take over my dad's business."

He moved his hand away, but he seemed to be waiting for her answer, so she nodded to confirm that she really meant it. Anyway, he wasn't making sense. It shouldn't matter what she thought unless— No, she couldn't leap to that conclusion. Not yet. She needed to hear him out and then decide how to react to what he'd said.

Kyle continued, seemingly oblivious to the ledge on which her heart was balanced. "Because I turned down my dad's offer last night to take over the business. I said goodbye to the potential big paycheck, too, though it didn't hurt as much as I expected it would.

"I think Dad was shocked that I turned it down after the campaign I staged to prove to him I could handle it. It's strange how sometimes you want something so badly until you get it. Then you realize it isn't what you wanted at all."

Julia found she couldn't relate. Only when she'd lost him had she realized he was the one person who could fill all the empty places inside her heart. Still, she was Kyle's friend first and would choose to be no matter what else happened between them. "What do you want to do more than run the business?"

"I want to be with you."

Julia's breath caught, and she blinked back the tears that suddenly clouded her eyes. If his words hadn't surprised her enough, his hands closed over hers and he partially rose from the table, leaning forward so he could touch his lips to hers.

He lifted his mouth a breath away but only so he could whisper the words, "I love you," before he kissed her once more. A moment of timeless perfection, it could neither be repeated nor would she ever desire it to. Julia would carefully fold it like a handkerchief and tuck it in the cedar chest of her memories.

When the kiss ended, Kyle pressed his cheek to Julia's, his warmth radiating through her skin.

Julia was the first to pull away. "Wait."

Kyle looked up at her, blinking in surprise. "What?"

"Is *being with me* all you plan to do now that you won't be working for your dad?"

"Why? Are you worried I'm going to be a freeloader?"

"I'm *trusting* that you might," she said with a grin.

Kyle sat in his chair again, dropping his shoulders in an exaggerated sigh. "I've created a monster."

He shook his head and smiled across the table at her. "I guess you have the right to know since this decision affects you. I want to work with convicts and ex-cons. You know, people who have a lot to prove, like I did. Like I still do. I want them to know they're not alone on their long road toward absolution."

"Oh, Kyle, that's great. I'm so pleased for you. I just knew getting the prison ministry off the ground would never be enough for you." She smiled at his shocked face. "I probably wasn't the only one who saw how perfect you were for that ministry."

Kyle tilted his head back and forth as if weighing her comment. "I guess Reverend Bob didn't seem that surprised when I called him late last night to tell him I wanted to stick with the ministry long-term. He seemed to think now that there's been an arrest in the series of church break-ins that securing widespread ecumenical, financial support will be a cinch. I'll actually be on staff at Hickory Ridge as a junior minister."

"What arrest? I haven't heard anything about any arrest." She'd listened to the rest of what Kyle had said, but that particular comment was the most critical. If an arrest had been made, Kyle would no longer be under suspicion, and she wanted that so much for him.

"It's true. Brett came to tell me himself since he says my help on the investigation resulted in the arrest." He was beaming as he told her how proud his family had been of him.

Julia reached across the table and gripped his

hands. "You see, Kyle. God did have a plan here. For all of us. He chose you for the prison ministry, and He used the rest of us to help guide you to your calling. He even used you to help solve the crimes."

"He had a plan, all right. He wanted me to meet you."

His fingers still loosely touching her hands, Kyle slid across the table and then kneeled in front of her chair.

"Julia Sims, I love you. I want to be with you always." He leaned forward and kissed the backs of her hands by turns before he pulled his head back and stared into her eyes. "Will you marry me? We'll probably have to live like pair of church mice for a while, and I can't even afford to get you an engagement ring right now, but one day—"

"I don't need an engagement ring, and I don't want only *one day,* either," she said, purposely misunderstanding him. "I want days and months and years with you. Yes, I'll marry you."

"You're an answer to all my best prayers," he whispered, his voice filled with emotion.

Standing, he pulled her to her feet and into his arms. His kiss was one of commitment, and Julia had the strangest sensation of being away a long time and finally finding her way home. She slid her hands over his triceps and across his shoulders, sinking her fingertips into the wisps of wavy hair at his nape.

His hair had grown a lot during the three months she'd known him, and she liked it longer like this.

The side of Kyle's mouth lifted as he pulled away from her and took her hands. Using his index finger, he drew an imaginary ring around the fourth finger of her left hand where he would someday place a wedding band. Julia could imagine it there already, the shining gold circle making a statement to all about the vows they'd made.

When Kyle looked up at her, he frowned. "Are you sure you won't be disappointed to be the wife of a poor junior minister?"

She shook her head at him and rolled her eyes. "I wouldn't have it any other way."

He just didn't get it: she would happily live her married life with him on the inside of a refrigerator box as long as they could be together.

Tilting his head to the side, he glanced at her again. "You never told me how you suddenly became confident that you could trust me. What changed?"

"I had a lot of time to think," she said with a shrug. "I had time to think about my own family and the things inside me that were keeping me from being able to love you the way I wanted to."

"Sounds like some heavy thinking."

"I prayed a lot, too. And I even received some advice from an unlikely source."

"Who?"

"Laura Sims."

"Really?" His eyes widened. "There has to be a story in there somewhere."

"There is. Laura has learned a lot about forgiveness, so maybe she was just the person to be able to tell me that in time you could forgive me, too."

"That's not one I would have predicted, but then the Lord does work in mysterious ways, doesn't He?"

Julia nodded. "If we let Him, God will find a way to use all of us."

Kyle grinned as he pulled his new fiancée in his arms again. "I think He's chosen me to become an incredible husband for one Julia Sims." He paused long enough brush his lips across hers, his smile remaining firmly in place. "And I'm ready to step up for the job."

Epilogue

A gust of September wind lifted the edges of the secured plastic tablecloths in the Central Park shelter, leaving a few leaves and a pile of pastel-colored "Julia and Kyle" napkins strewn all over the cement floor.

Julia grinned as she watched Serena Westin, Charity McKinley, Tricia Lancaster and Hannah McBride scatter as quickly at the leaves in their tea-length, mint-colored bridesmaid dresses, capturing all of the napkins except for the ones that Julia's niece, Grace, had nabbed first. Those were wadded into balls in Grace's attempt to "help." The others wouldn't be pristinely clean, but that would add to the picniclike quality of the park wedding.

"Now, you see, Julia," Laura Sims said, clucking her tongue. "I warned you that an outdoor wedding might be a risk this late in the season."

"Don't worry, Laura," Julia told her with a smile. It still felt strange to refer to the other woman by her first name, but she was beginning to get used to doing it. "There's not a cloud in the sky. It's going to be a perfect end-of-summer day."

Technically, she couldn't even call it summer anymore, but she and Kyle didn't want to wait until next summer to become husband and wife, so they'd hurried the wedding plans and had stretched the season by a week.

"It would have been so much easier to have the ceremony inside the church," Laura mumbled.

"Mother," Charity said, resting a hand on Laura's shoulder. "You promised to be on your best behavior today."

Laura opened her mouth to retort, but Julia waved her hand between them to keep the peace.

"She's fine, Charity," Julia assured her before turning back to her sister's mother. "I know it would have been easier there, but I want to thank you so much for helping me to put on my wedding here. I don't know what I would have done without you since my own mom and dad—" She cleared her throat to remove the lump there.

"Well, anyway. Thanks. I just love this place. It feels like God is watching over us here. And besides, Kyle and I have some great memories here, too."

They'd had their first fight here…and their first

kiss. And now they would share their first day as husband and wife here under the same sky, with the already changing trees and the Huron River providing the perfect backdrop for a picture God had painted himself. The site was slightly different today, with rows of brown folding chairs, a music stand and a couple of flower stands borrowed from the church, but it still couldn't have been a more perfect place for her and Kyle to begin their new life together.

Charity stepped forward then, taking charge as she often did, but this time in her capacity as matron of honor. "Now enough of that, little sister, or you'll mess up that makeup I just worked so hard on. You look beautiful, and I want to keep it that way." She handed Julia her simple bouquet of pink roses.

Julia did feel beautiful in her silk wedding gown, its strapless silhouette unadorned but for the beaded band that formed its low waistline. With the wind as strong as it had been today, she was glad she'd opted to skip the veil and to clip her hair at her nape rather than to fight both during the ceremony.

"It's almost time, ladies," Mary Nelson called as she hurried into the shelter, a pile of programs still in her hands. "Reverend Bob's already up there."

"Are you feeling all right, Mary?" Julia couldn't help asking. "You've looked flushed ever since you arrived."

"No, I'm fine," Mary assured her.

But when the sweet, older woman lifted a hand

to her face, a modest diamond engagement ring winked out at them.

"You're engaged!" Julia exclaimed, hurrying over to hug the minister's new fiancée. "Why didn't you tell us?"

"Yeah, why didn't you tell *me?*" Hannah said with a frown before she took her turn hugging Mary. She hadn't made it a secret that she'd long wanted her father to marry this woman who was already honorary grandmother to her daughters.

"Bob just asked last night," Mary explained. "And I didn't want to take away from Julia's special day."

"You've just added to it," Julia assured her. "You're going to make Reverend Bob very happy. I know it."

Colleen Lancaster crossed the shelter then, her forest-green dress flowing behind her. "The ushers want me to sit, but I wanted to come kiss both of my daughters-in-law first."

She kissed Tricia and Julia and then hurried back to the line, so that Brett could usher her to her seat. Julia was so pleased Kyle had chosen his brother as best man. It was another sign that forgiveness and new beginnings really were possible.

All the bridesmaids lined up and started down the aisle created from a roll of white paper. As the first in the procession, Hannah held hands with flower girl Grace, who held a basket of daisies that she emptied long before she'd reached Reverend Bob. The others followed, and then it was Julia's turn.

"Ready for this?" her brother-in-law, Rick, asked as the processional music on the CD player changed. He held out his arm to escort her down the aisle.

"I can't wait," Julia said with a smile.

Only when her sister had made it all the way to the front and had turned off to the left did Julia get her first good look at Kyle. He was so handsome in his black wedding suit and black tie, the only color a pink rose boutonniere pinned at his lapel.

His gaze was so intense and warm that Julia's face and neck heated with a flush. She'd never felt more beautiful or more loved. *Thank you, God.* She didn't even bother listing the things she was grateful for in her prayer; there were too many to enumerate.

As soon as Rick and Julia reached the front, where Reverend Bob stood and all the others waited, Kyle surprised her by leaning close.

"I love you, Julia," he whispered before dropping a kiss on her lips.

"Hey, wait a minute," Reverend Bob said, his frown quickly turning to a grin. "You're supposed to wait until the end for that."

Kyle shrugged. "Oh, sorry. I've never been much of a rule follower."

"You can say that again," Brett chimed in, elbowing his brother in the side.

Kyle elbowed him back before turning to face the minister again. "But I'll kiss her then, too. That is, if you insist."

The crowd that had begun snickering at the kiss was full-out laughing by this point. Reverend Bob had to quiet them down before he could begin reading the vows. Julia was having a hard time listening to what he was saying, anyway. She was too busy being lost in the eyes of the man she loved. Kyle never looked away from her, and Julia didn't want to see anything else but his face.

She focused on the words that Reverend Bob read from First Corinthians Chapter 13, about love being patient and kind. She'd already seen those things played out in so many ways. When the minister reached the part that said, "love conquers all," she couldn't think of a truer statement.

For them, love had had a lot to conquer—the sins of Kyle's past, the scars of hers. Their journey leading them together had been a long one, as well, with many wrong turns and detours. But the peace so clear in Kyle's eyes mirrored the feeling deep in her heart: they'd both found their way home.

* * * * *

Dear Reader,

Homecoming—that word brings back so many great adolescent memories for me. I am reminded of football games on frosty Indiana nights and huge church picnics on sunny summer afternoons. Through events like those, we visited with our past by allowing friends whose journeys have led them elsewhere the chance to come home.

The whole idea of home appeals to me, as well— its warmth, protectiveness and sense of belonging. In *Homecoming at Hickory Ridge,* Kyle must find his way home, but I believe that many moments in our lives as Christians are about going home, from the first moment we choose to have a relationship with God to the day we leave this earth. No matter how far we've traveled from Him, our God, like the man in the Parable of the Prodigal Son, opens His arms and welcomes us home.

I love hearing from readers and may be contacted through my Web site at www.danacorbit.com or by regular mail at P.O. Box 2251, Farmington Hills, MI 48333-2251.

Dana Corbit

QUESTIONS FOR DISCUSSION

1. Helping people is an integral part of Julia Sims's personality and part of the reason she chose a career in teaching. Name some of the other "projects" she undertakes to help others.

2. One of the primary themes in this story is "coming home." What are some of the varied ways the author dealt with this concept? In what ways can church communities provide a "home" for their members?

3. Julia has been set up several times through the church's singles' program, but none of those matchups have resulted in a romance. What are some of the reasons why all of those plans failed?

4. Part of Kyle's character journey involves his efforts to restore his relationships with his family. He relates his experience to the Parable of the Prodigal Son. How is Kyle's story like that of the prodigal, and how is it different?

5. One of Kyle's harshest critics is his own brother, Brett, the police officer who is ashamed to be related to an ex-con. Why are we some-

times most critical of the people closest to us, those we should love the most?

6. Initially, Kyle considers the job working with the church's prison ministry as a stepping stone where he can prove himself to his father and earn a position in the family business. What about seeing his father makes Kyle rethink his goal?

7. What are some things Kyle does to prove to his family that he has changed? How does he grow as a character?

8. Kyle worries about how the people will react to him after learning he has a prison record, but he has a bigger problem with his past than almost anyone else does. Why can Christians easily accept God's forgiveness and still find it difficult to forgive themselves?

9. Andrew Westin tells Kyle that Mary Nelson is good for Reverend Bob after his last disastrous relationship. What went wrong in that relationship, and what makes Mary a good partner for him?

10. Kyle's step-nephew, Max, easily accepts him as "Uncle Kyle" and plays a role in bringing

him into the family. What can children teach us about loving as God loves us?

11. What is the one thing that Kyle needs from a relationship, and why is it that Julia can't give him that one thing? What is most important to you in a relationship?

12. Why is it ironic that Laura Sims serves as Julia's confidante when Julia feels there's no hope for restoring her relationship with Kyle? And what is ironic about Julia being the person who helps lead Laura to an honest relationship with God?

13. Julia and her half sister, Charity, were both betrayed in different ways by their parents. How did their parents betray them, and how did they each respond to that betrayal?

14. What does Julia finally discover is behind her need to fix other people? Do you know anyone who reaches out to others when she really needs to address the pain within herself?

Love Inspired® SUSPENSE

RIVETING INSPIRATIONAL ROMANCE

Watch for our new series of
edge-of-your-seat suspense novels.
These contemporary tales
of intrigue and romance
feature Christian characters
facing challenges to their faith...
and their lives!

Steeple Hill®

Visit:
www.SteepleHill.com